DADDY'S DREAM

DADDY'S DREAM

DADDY'S DREAM

Novel

Kevin B. Anderson

ANDERSON BOOK PUBLISHING
NEWPORT NEWS, VIRGINIA

DADDY'S DREAM

Published by:
Anderson Book Publishing
Newport New, Virginia
Email: kevluv21@gmail.com

Kevin Anderson, Publisher / Editorial Director
Yvonne Rose/Quality Press.Info, Book Packager
Formatted By: Mychea, Inc

ISBN: 978-0-692-51746-8

Library of Congress Control Number: 2015950537

DEDICATION

Dedicated to my mother Mary Bostic and to my children:
Kevin J.A. Anderson, Anthony S. Anderson, Kaniya B. Anderson, Shaquille
Serrette and a special dedication to my other mother Jennette Jones

ACKNOWLEDGEMENTS

First, I'd like to give thanks and praise to God for giving me the wisdom and strength to carry out this project.

I would like to say thank you to my father, George Anderson for opening my eyes and mind to the world of literature.

I would like to say thank you to Amber Books for helping me with my first book. Looking forward to doing more work with you guys.

Shout out to my lil brother Kenny Kendoggs Peele, who is serving time in Auburn Correctional.

Shout out to my extended family: Jean Parker and children: Bill, Jay, Marty, Reese, Kim, Keisha, Nita, Katrice, Regina, Sheryl and my brother Robert (Hopp) Parker... stay gold!!!

Shout out to my sweetheart Erica Perkins and family Mel, Kierra, Kayla.

Shout out to all my cousins: Nate Bostic, Andre Bostic, Veronica Bostic, and Kenyatta the one I still look up to since I can remember as a little boy Gregory Brown another one of my cousins, who I admire. He is currently serving time in Sing Correctional Facility.

Shout out to my cousin June and Corrine, Darryl and Claudine; and Aunt Martha Frenda, Lin and daughter Lisa.

Shout out to Vince Bostic. Shout out to my Auntie Sybil Hopkins. Shout out to my Richmond peeps, Poochie, to my brother from another mother Haywood Poindexter; shout out to my boy, who I call Jelly, and Dog; shout out to my Norfolk brother, Blanco.

Shout out to my old hood: Gates Ave Bedstuy, Brooklyn, N A Rock. Shout to Kingston Ave - Nikki, Drew, Bradly, Jen Jen, Stefanie (PEENIE), Mary, Petey, and Na Na. Shout out to Yonkers, NY - Wendy Derry, Coco, Jojo, and D-Block.

Shout to my Newport News people: Keda, Flashlight, Trina, Lil Hershey, Kake, Rizzy, and Mckiense. Shout out to Morgan Moses. Shout out to my sister Michelle Bradley. Shout out to my sister Kiva. Shout out to Sage, my niece and to Demetria Peele. Shout out to Sheree Brooks and my lil super, Keria Brooks. Shout out to my barber, KB from Unique Styled.

Shout out to Lorraine Synder (community access). Shout out to my cousin/brother David Brown, who introduced me to Sound of Music. Thanks cuz. Shout out to my boxing trainer Lloyd. Shout out to my niece Jennifer. Nephew Byron, Anthony and all the others. Ray Ray, Niece Robin and Rissa. JaJa. Shout out to Silk and Meedy. Silk who iz a dj has radio time on www.b.radio. Shout out to my friend Wayne Johnson, Sandy and Tasha from Carlton Ave.

I wanna give a special shout out to Arlene Serrette, my Trinidad dream. U R truly a ruby, thanks for your support!!!!! If I forgot anyone, it was not my intention. God Bless!!!!!!

ONE

DADDY WAS listening to one of his favorite cd's when the dispatcher beeped in.

"Car seven? Give me your location." The owner of We Can Get You There wanted all drivers to be addressed by car number because he thought that was being professional.

"I'm on the North Side. Why? Wassup?"

"Good. Can you pick up a customer? She's at 1520 Bedford Ave, and she's going to 50 West St."

Damn, Daddy thought. 50 West Street? Damn! That's in Manhattan. "Okay. Tell her I'll be there in 10 minutes."

I know Brooklyn like I know my name, Daddy thought, *so it won't take long to get to 1520 Bedford Ave, but damn, Manhattan? Shit! He didn't feel like driving over the bridge today. Oh well, fuck it.* Daddy pulled up in front of 1520 Bedford Ave and saw the most beautiful woman he had ever laid eyes on.

"Excuse me miss. Did you call for a cab service?" He sure hoped she said yes.

"Are you from We Can Get You There?"

"Yep. That would be me"

She got into the car, and instantly I smelled lilacs and roses, like she was born around flowers because she smelled just like that! Flowers.

"Good morning, Miss. 50 West Street, right?"

"Yes, please! Thank you and good morning to you, too."

Damn she smelled good. Was that perfume she had on or body lotion? He hoped it was body lotion because he liked that better. He took a glance at her through the mirror and quickly turned his eyes back on the road when her eyes looked back. *Damn! She is so beautiful.* So Daddy, feeling himself this morning, started to sing, something on the top of his head. It sounded so good the passenger thought it was the radio.

"Who is that? Can you turn that up?"

Daddy laughed. "Umm that's me," he said, pleased that she was saying something to him.

"That's you? Wow! You sound so good. What was that you were singing?"

"Something I just made up"

"Well, can you sing that again? It sounded really good."

Daddy sang a little more of the song that had won her ear. Looking at her enjoying what she was hearing, he had almost run into a bus. He put on the breaks just in time. "Damn! Close one"

"Yes," she said. "That was close. But wow! You got an amazing voice."

"I wouldn't say all that." Daddy replied.

"No seriously. I have heard people on the radio who can't even come close to what you got. You ever tried to use it professionally?"

"No, I can't say that I have."

2

"So what are you waiting for? You could be doing that instead of Driving Miss Daisy."

He laughed at the little joke. West Street was about 20 minutes away and he wished that it was two more hours instead of 20 minutes, 'cause the way he was feeling and what Miss Daisy was saying was filling his head up with good stuff. He did not want this to end. No one had appreciated his voice the way she had. No one had made him feel like he wanted to sing just because. In a huge way she inspired him.

"Well, Miss Daisy. We are almost there."

She laughed when he called her that remembering her little joke earlier. "And it was a beautiful experience as well as a safe ride."

"Thank you," he replied.

"No! Thank you, Mr. Singer! You really took me somewhere singing like that."

They were in front of the destination, and he wanted to say a lot more than telling her how much the fare was, but it was against the rules to come on to a passenger, as an earlier situation with another driver had made that rule happen.

"That will be fifteen dollars," he had told her.

To his astonishment, she handed him the fare along with her card. I know some people who would just love to hear you, if you are interested. I'm not trying to push anything on you, but if you have a voice like that to offer the world, then why not go for it, right?"

Daddy looked at the card, then turned around and looked at her. "So you are an editor?"

"Yes. I work for City Newspaper."

"Wow! That's good! It must be exciting to work for a newspaper."

"It has its rewards," she said. "I gotta run." I hope you decide to call. I would love for you to meet my people."

"I will. I will."

They shook hands, and he didn't want to let go, for the softness of her hand had him stuck.

"Can I have my hand back please? I need it to do some typing."

"Of course, my bad. I forgot I still had it."

Smiling, she said, "Have a nice day." And with that, she got out of the car and started walking to the building. Still parked there, he looked at her walking, so sexy, into the building. Sensing that he was still there, she turned halfway around and waved, holding her cell phone up saying, "Call me!"

He waved back saying "I will" as if she could hear him. Then she disappeared.

Jasmine. Jasmine Green. That's a nice name, he said to himself. *And Damn! How am I gonna say I forgot I still had it. What a knucklehead! Was I that caught up by the softness of her touch to say something stupid like that?*

As Daddy drove back to Brooklyn, he could not stop thinking about Jasmine and everything she was saying. Here was a beautiful woman telling him that he had the most amazing voice she had heard. *Cindy never told me that. And I sing around the house all the time, especially in the shower.*

Cindy! Fuck! That's all she was, a good fuck. For six months she has been living with me, and for six months it has been pain and pleasure: Pleasure because of her sexuality; pain because of her personality. She was definitely one I couldn't take to eat Sunday dinner at Mamado's house. It just wouldn't seem like the right thing to do.

Now Jasmine, she is for sure an apple pie at Mamado's house on the porch after dinner kinda girl. She could hold the right conversation at the right time. Man! Why was he still thinking about her? Was it because he just left her? Or *was it because she seemed like the girl who has been in my dreams ever since I can remember?*

I wonder if she has a boyfriend, Daddy thought to himself. *She's not married because I noticed no ring on her finger. An editor of an established newspaper. What could she possibly see in one who drives for a living? Not to mention the hustling!* He wasn't no big time drug dealer. Not like his boy Peanuts. But all the same, he was in the streets. And she didn't fit the description of one who likes bad boys.

Daddy was back in Brooklyn within no time, still in deep thought about the beautiful woman he had just dropped off. He was driving down New York Avenue when he saw his boy, Peanuts. So he pulled over to holla' at him.

"Peanuts! Yo, Peanuts! What up my nigga?"

"Yo! What up kid! Still playin' Taxi, I see."

"Yep! And I just finished drivin' your momma down to the strip club so she wouldn't be late for work!"

"Fuck you nigga!" They both laughed, gave each other dap, and hugged.

"So, what you into this mornin', Peanuts?"

Peanuts and Daddy had been friends for as long as they could remember. Peanuts got his name 'cause you always saw him eating them. So Daddy nicknamed him that, and ever since then everybody was calling him that. It fit because every time nowadays, when he was to buy something that seemed expensive, he would say that, "Peanuts," meaning that the price didn't mean nothing to him 'cause he had dough.

"I'm not into shit, my nigga'. Just doin' what I do. You know me. Gettin' that bread!"

"Aye yo. I met this honey that would remind you of Selena Jordan, word to mother kid! She was drop dead beautiful!"

"Word!" Peanuts said. "So did you get her number?"

"What's my name, what's my name? My name is Daddy kid! Of course I got the digits! I wouldn't even be telling you about her if I didn't."

"Alright, alright! So did you call her yet?"

"Naw, I just met her this morning. You know I gotta' play my mack right. I'll give it a few days."

"Don't let Cindy find out. You know that broad ain't having that!"

"There you go. Gotta' fuck my morning up just by bringing her damn name up. I'm tired of her ass, word up yo! She always beefing. All the bitch do is strip. And I supposed to do this and do that. I'm always spending on her. Sometimes I think she only with me 'cause of dat. And she always talking about my car."

"She do gotta point, tho Kid. It's 2007 and you still driving that old ass car!"

"Man, fuck that shit! I ain't got it like that to be drivin' no Benz like you."

"I told you before, you could get you one too, just fuck wit me!"

"Naw, I'm good. I'm not doin' that shit full time. I'm not tryin' to get hemmed up, get caught, and do some time."

"Nigga! You hustling now, so why not do it big? Get some real money and that's that!"

"Naw, I'm getting ready to stop the little bit I'm doing now and get into something else."

"Alright, Kid. I'm just saying. I'm here if you change your mind."

"No doubt. I got you. Let me get back to work."

"Alright, Kid."

After the conversation with Peanuts, Mike was on his way home from work. Sometimes he didn't want to go there, but hell! That was his house; he paid the bills. Cindy had moved in with him, not him with her. So he felt that he should come home to something pleasant and peaceful. Instead there was nothing but lust and lies; not love, which he wanted.

He didn't like the way Cindy carried on about him not having a better car. *What was wrong with this one? It wasn't no Benz, but damn! It gets you to your destination, don't it? Yeah! We gotta' have a talk when I get home. We definitely gonna talk.*

He pulls up to his house, ready for a confrontation with The Spider Woman, but no matter what, she always seems to win.

"Hey, Baby! How was your day?" Cindy asked.

"It was alright. And yours?"

"It was alright. I feel I got something done. I did some studying, trying to get ready for this test."

"Cindy, I wanna talk to you."

"About what, Daddy?" she asked, climbing up on his lap.

He hated moments like this. Every time he wanted to get his point across, she would distract him.

"Oh, about…" and that was all he could say, 'cause she had her tongue all down his throat making him swallow the conversation that he wanted to have with her, along with the juices that came from her succulent kiss. If Cindy knew anything, she knew how to get him hard, and right now he was concrete brick hard! She moaned by the passion of her own lovemaking to him.

Daddy was so intoxicated by her scent that it drove him crazy and he just ripped her blouse open. That led to a world of pleasure. He took hold of her breast both with his hand and his tongue.

Cindy, who herself was lost in the sex that was taking place, started whispering in his ear (which he loved). "I want that dick inside me. I want JoJo inside me."

He liked it when she called his dick by name. That just made him more excited. "I'm gonna fuck the shit outta you, bitch!"

"Damn! I love it when you call me that. Fuck me Nigga! Fuck me!"

Daddy already had his pants off. And when he stuck JoJo inside of her that was all she wrote. It was like they were having sex all day, 'cause Cindy instantly came. And she came right on his dick, the warm juices creaming all over his dick made it even harder. So she jumped off and put all of it in her mouth. Sucking him off like her life depended on it and caressing his nipples at the same time. Daddy could do nothing but be under her spell. She was looking up at him while she was jamming JoJo down her throat waiting for him to come, which should be any second. Daddy himself, intense with the thrill he was getting ready to experience, was looking deep into her eyes as if that was the magic that held him captive.

"Ima bust all in your mouth. Damn bitch! Damn!" When he came, he collapsed. "Damn!"

Smiling, Cindy stood up and said, "Now what was that you wanted to talk about?"

"Naw! Nothing, not now. Now right now."

And that's the way it always happened. Every time he needed to talk. He didn't or he couldn't.

"Daddy, I need a fur coat and some new boots."

"You need a fur coat or you want a fur coat? I don't think a person *needs* a fur coat, Cindy."

"Need! Want! It's the same thing."

"No it's not. You don't need a fur coat when I just fucking bought you a Northface last week."

"So what? I didn't ask for you to buy me that coat. You did that on your own. It's nice, I like it, but I want a fur coat. So why can't you get me one? You got the money to get me one."

"Wait a minute. Hold on. You mean to tell me I come in here, ain't shit cooked. You hop on my lap, fuck my brains loose and all of a sudden I'm supposed to buy you a fur coat? Bitch, please!"

"For one, I told you I don't cook. And second, you didn't have a problem when I was fucking and sucking your ass, and third, my friend Shay-Shay got one. Peanuts bought her a diamond necklace and a fur coat. I'm not asking for both, just the fur coat."

"Oh, so now I get it. Just because Peanuts bought Sha-Shay one, I'm supposed to do the same. Fuck that shit! I'm not getting' no fur coat."

"Oh yes you is, motherfucker. Watch, yes you is!"

"Now I'm a motherfucker. See what I mean? You always on some bullshit. No matter how much I do, you always bitching about what we don't have. If it's not my car it's this apartment. If it's not this, it's that. Why I always gotta go through this with you."

"Mike." She always called him by his birth name when they was arguing. "Here it is, and you have an old ass Honda Accord and you got the nerve to even put 20s on it." Hahaha! Cindy was laughing and she couldn't stop.

"You have no problem getting in it though, do you? I come pick your strippin' ass up and drop you off, don't I?"

"Fuck you, nigga! Fuck you nig-ga! There are plenty niggas wanting this, and they got good sense to know what they have, I bet. So fuck you again, Mike!"

"Hey, do what you do Ma! The door is right there if you gotta bring other niggas into this. Go let them buy you a fur coat, 'cause I'm not!"

"Forget your stingy ass." Cindy slammed the door, took out her phone and called Shay-Shay.

Shay-Shay was Peanuts' main lady. Even though she knew Peanuts was messing around, she didn't care about that. All she cared about was him being safe in the streets. It was a cruel world out there. And she didn't wanna' lose him to it. Ring! Ring! Ring!

Shay Reached for her phone. "Hello? Oh what up, Girl?"

"Can you come get me? I need to get out this fucking house!"

"Why? What happened?"

"'Cause I can't stand this stingy ass nigga."

"Oh boy! What's going on with you two? Wow!"

"Just come get me, please!"

"Okay, okay! Calm down. I'll be there in a second."

TWO

MAD AS hell, Daddy took off into the streets to let some steam out of him. He didn't believe in striking a girl, but he wanted to choke the shit out of her. And not for what had just taken place. It was built up anger for every time she started something. For every time she would down him for what he wasn't or what he didn't have.

Fuck! Why me? Why do I have to put up with this shit all the time?

He got into his car and drove off. Driving gave him a sense of escape. He could drive for hours. When something was on his mind and he didn't feel like being bothered, he would get into his car and just drive anywhere.

And music! Boy did he love music, especially R&B. He could sound just like most of the male singers. Listening to an old Marvin Gaye CD made him think about that lovely woman he had dropped off in Manhattan this morning. What was it about her that kept him thinking of her?

Jasmine. He should call her. Naw, then she would think he was desperate. But then again, he didn't have to be calling her like he wanted to ask her to go out with him or something like that. She did give him her number 'cause she felt that she could help him. *She said she knew somebody that would like my singing.* So maybe he could call her and make that the excuse.

Naw, I'll wait," he decided. *Maybe this weekend I'll call.*

❀   ❀   ❀

JASMINE GREEN was beautiful. Men and women alike would tell her this, but she felt different inside. In fact, she felt ugly.

People would say things like, "Wow! You should be in a magazine," or "Go for modeling or something 'cause you sure have a face that would be the talk of the entertainment world!"

But she knew that they were all lies. The truth was that she was so ugly, that she hated looking in the mirror. For the secret that she had kept hidden in her memory had her live out the truth for years. She had held on to her secret 'cause she swore to the person that had made her a woman that she would never say a word.

"Jasmine? Jasmine?"

"Oh! Yes Miss Johnson?"

"Child, where are you? I have been calling you for the past 2 minutes and you seemed like you were in a daze or something!"

"Sorry, Miss Johnson. I…"

"No problem, Sweetie. I understand. He must be something else to have you daydreaming like that."

"Huh? Oh no, Miss Johnson. I was thinking about work," she lied.

"Yeah, okay. Whatever you say, Sweetheart. Anyway, I was calling you because it's going on 6:00. Why don't you pack up and get ready to go home and start your weekend. You work so hard."

"Ok, Miss Johnson. I just want to finish my last page."

"Okay. I'm gone. Don't forget to lock up and have a great weekend."

"Okay, I won't. And you too!"

Jasmine thought to herself, *Wow, embarrassing! My boss caught me daydreaming. Was I lost that much in my thoughts?*

Not only could she visualize his face while she was daydreaming, but she could hear his voice and the song he was singing this morning. *That man had a voice on him! And handsome! Boy! Was he handsome!* She thought to herself. His face had features that she couldn't put into words. *And his eyes, Oh my God! A girl could lose her breath looking into them.*

I wonder should I tell Tricia about him. No because all she is gonna do is say, "So, did you get his number?" or "Is you gonna date him?" and so on.

She didn't even know his name. *He probably won't call anyway, even though I told him that I knew someone that would love to hear his voice; someone that could help him get into the music world.*

Oh well. If he don't call, it's no biggie. Even though I wouldn't mind seeing him again. Surprised that she had thought that long about the stranger with the voice, she smiled, shook her head, locked up everything, and looked forward to the great weekend that Miss Johnson had told her to have.

DADDY WAS on his way back home from driving around the city. He had calmed down and had realized that he was hungry. So he stopped by the Chinese diner and ordered two dinners: One for him and one for Cindy. Even though they had just had an argument, he brought her a dinner because he was used to doing that. After all, she was his girl, right? She had to eat also; if she didn't want it, it was on her. He had done his part. Why couldn't she just chill and support him the way he wanted her to. That's all he asked.

She should be home, he had said to himself, and he hoped to God that it was different when he got there. He didn't want any more stress. His phone rang. It was a weekend customer. His regular.

Damn, he thought. *It's Friday. And I don't even have no goods! See what I mean? Arguing with this damn fool and I forgot to re-up.*

He answered the call and told the customer that he wasn't good, but he will be in a couple of hours. The customer said, "Damn, okay," and he hung up.

"I've got to do better!" Daddy said. "This shit here ain't workin' out. I mean, I make a little money, but I don't need that stress neither. I don't see how Peanuts put up with it!"

Daddy walked into his house and all hope for not being stressed was gone.

"Hey Daddy Mike!" A voice yelled out that he could care less about hearing.

"Yeah, yeah, yeah. What's goin' on, Tricia?"

Tricia sucked her teeth and said, "Damn, that's how you feel? I didn't have to speak to you."

"It didn't matter if you did or not Tricia, trust me, when I tell you." Daddy put the Chinese food on the table.

"Chinese, Chinese, Chinese. Damn," Cindy said. It feels like I'm in a Kung Fu movie. We eat so much of this shit. Why your cheap ass couldn't go to the Steak & Shrimp Stop or something?"

"If you don't want the food, then don't eat it. Just don't say nothin' else to me please!"

"Dag," Tricia said. "Why you got to be so egotistical?"

"Tricia, please!" Daddy said with disgust. "You don't even know how to spell the word. So shut the hell up!"

"Don't talk to my friend like that!"

"You and your friend both could get the hell out of my house!"

"No, you get the hell out, 'cause we ain't going nowhere! How 'bout that?"

"It's okay, Girl. I was just leaving anyway. I got some things to take care of.

"Aight Girl. I'll call you later".

"Aight. Later Daddy Mike. Mister Egotistical man."

He hated when she called him Daddy Mike. It was like she was being funny or something.

"Yea, yea. Bye."

"Why you gotta be that way towards my company?"

"What the hell you talking about? I walk in my house and was gonna try and make things up, but instead I walk in to a male bashing club."

"So how was you gonna' make things up? I don't see no fur coat?"

"Let's not go there again."

"Let's not go there, let's not go there. Nigga, we never left from there. Mike you are so fucking cheap, it's a shame. All of my girls got a fur coat except me."

"Is this relationship based on money and material?" Daddy asked.

"Every time I ask you to buy me something, you ask that lame ass question."

"It's true, Cindy. You don't do nothing else but complain and demand this and that. You don't even give me support in anything I do. I could see if you were having my back on things, being my backbone. You laugh when I tell you about my dreams."

"Mike, you wanna be an R&B singer. That is whack. I could see if you sayin' you wanted to rap, but sing? Please! You are a product of the hood. They either sell drugs or get into the hip hop game 'cause that is where the money is."

"Is that all you care about is money?"

"How else we gonna live? Money is the source to a whole lot of things. So if you think I'm all about money, maybe I am. So take me or leave me."

"Don't tempt me," Daddy responded.

"I know niggas that want this pussy. So I don't care if you're tempted or not. But trust me, you'll miss this ass! Believe that!"

Daddy couldn't argue with that. She sure did know how to turn him on; and like the bitch had said, he would miss her sexy ass. But for some reason, he didn't trust her.

DADDY HAD strange feelings about his relationship with Cindy. They'd had arguments before, but for her to go on about this fur coat thing was too much. He knew the women was devious, but the way she had sounded was that he had better get her one, or else! And she always threw that she knew niggas who want her in his face, as if to say she had someone on the side already.

That girl is crazy, Daddy said to himself as he drove to his connect to re-up. *I should just end this relationship, 'cause it's not getting me nowhere. I don't need the headache. And I could get sex without attachment, so why do I have someone living with me who doesn't have my best interest at heart? And why would she tell me I ain't worth shit if she know I got money to buy her a fur coat (which I do).*

See, that bitch is confused. Maybe it was her way of getting her way. Like telling a brother he ain't shit and he goes out and prove to her that he is. But fuck that! He didn't have to prove shit to her and nobody else.

Singing is whack. What the hell does she know?

See what I mean? No support. Whatever happened to ... ? "Damn. Baby! That's good that you wanna sing." And "I love your singing.*

Yeah, maybe it was time to end this relationship. But how?

His phone started ringing. *Damn my phone is ringing off the hook. I know it's Friday, but damn, these dope heads can't wait.*

He picked up the phone and smiled when he recognized the number.

"Hey, Mamado!"

"Hello, Son! And how are you these days. You don't call your mother, so I gotta call you and see how you doing."

"Sorry, Mamado! I just be busy."

"Michael Theodore Flowers Junior! You mean to tell me that you are too busy to call y our mother, not to mention stop by once in a blue!"

"Naw, Mamado! It's not like that. I just be tryin' hard to get my life straight."

"And you think being out in those streets is getting your life straight?"

Daddy was quiet on the phone asking himself, *how does she know what I do. I keep it away from her. At least I think I do.*

"What? Cat got your tongue?" his mother asked. "You don't think your mother knows her son? You need to come to church and sing for the Lord. God gave you that beautiful voice so that you can sing for Him. So you better use it before he takes it away. Boy! If your father was alive today, he'd be telling you the same thing."

Daddy's father, Michael Theodore Flowers Sr. had been killed in the Army in an explosion that took place in Pakistan. But he had been a hero saving two little children. He had gone back inside to

17

rescue another child, but the house had exploded. When Daddy, his mother and brother had heard the news, they were all devastated.

Daddy was 11 years old when that had happened. Not understanding death and why that had to be his family going through it, he had turned to the streets rebelling against the system that he thought was responsible for his father not being alive. Why did he have to be in the Army in the first place? Well, he sure as hell wasn't going into no Army.

"I know Mamado. I know. I'm, gonna come to church one day, if it would make you happy."

"Yes, Son! That would make me happy. But it's for you more than me. I want you to have a better life. And just maybe you might find yourself a good girl."

When his mother had said that, he thought of Jasmine. He wondered if she went to church.

"Yes, Mother a good girl. I'll find her." Or maybe he already had.

"Okay, Son. Mamado has to go. I was just calling to say Hello."

"Aight Mamado. I love you."

"I love you, too, Son."

When he hung up from his mother, he thought about what she was saying. A good girl. He thought about both Cindy and Jasmine and how different they were. Cindy didn't fit into his dream. And Jasmine was a dream. Yin and Yang. Totally different.

Daddy had picked up his goods from his connect who he had been dealing with for a moment now. It wasn't nothing major that he was getting from him. Just something to keep a little money coming in. He could have easily gotten his stuff from Peanuts, but he didn't want to mix business with friendship. He felt it was taboo.

❀　❀　❀

WHEN JASMINE got home, she was exhausted. She had worked hard this week. But that was the case every week at work. She loved working and she loved the work she did. Ever since college days, she had worked hard to get top grades. So working came easy. That's why she was good at what she did. In fact, she was one of the best editors in the city, and was in demand. She had graduated with flying colors in her English major. And that afforded her a position with the top newspaper in the city. They had loved her work instantly, as instantly as they had loved her. Everyone loved Jasmine Green. She had a kind spirit that you just warmed to. She always was polite and when you spoke to her, she would speak back with a smile that made the sun come out on a gloomy day.

She sat down on her futon, took off her shoes and gave her feet what they had been asking for all day long. Air! And just when she thought that she could sit there for a while, one of her closest friends, Spirit her cat, came up to her meowing and rubbing up against her, begging to be fed.

"Hey, Girl! You wanna eat, huh? I bet you are starved. Come on. Mommy gonna feed you right now."

She got up to feed Spirit and walking on the hard floor massaged her feet, and it felt so good. She gave Spirit her dinner and she dug into it like it was steak and eggs! Looking at Spirit eat her way to a lazy evening, she herself felt hungry. She didn't feel like cooking. She would order some Chinese food. She went to the phone to retrieve her messages. There were only a couple messages from telemarketers and one from Tricia.

"Hey Girl! I see you not home yet. I was just calling to see what you was doing this weekend. Call me when you get home."

I'll call her after I order my Chinese food. She got the Chinese menu and called in her regular.

"Hello? This is Miss Greene at 1520 Bedford Ave. I would like to place an order."

"Hello Miss Greene. I already know that's you. Do you want your regular rib tips and shrimp fried rice?"

Surprised and impressed, Jasmine said, "Yes! That's exactly what I want. And extra duck sauce please? Thank you."

Wok & Wok took pride in knowing their customers. It was a part of their service, especially when they were polite like Jasmine always was. Jasmine decided that she would call Tricia back later after she took a shower. So she went into her bathroom, ran the lukewarm water, and got undressed. She looked over and saw Spirit fast asleep.

She is so lazy, Jasmine thought to herself. Or maybe I just envy her right now, sleeping like that. Getting ready to get into the shower, she looked into the mirror at her body, asking the mirror if she was too thin or too fat. If the mirror was a guy, it would have told her that she had an amazing body, 'cuz that's just what her 5 feet 7 inch, butter pecan skin tone body was: Amazing!

She worked out at the gym and ran every morning before she went to work. She wasn't really doing it to maintain her fitness and good looks as much as she was doing it for staying healthy. When she got out of the shower, she lay across her bed with a towel under her and let the after effects of a massaging shower take over. And just as she was almost lost in her euphoric state, the doorbell rang. Not happy that her euphoria was broken, she quickly got up, threw on her robe, and went to the door. She knew it was the Chinese delivery man because she wasn't expecting anybody else. So she grabbed her wallet.

"How much do I owe you?"

"$9.50, Miss Greene," the delivery man replied.

"Okay, here's $11.00."

"Thank you, Miss Greene. Enjoy!"

She closed the door and sat everything on the kitchen table; but before she ate, she would return Tricia's call. She started to pick up the phone, but it rang before she could pick it up. It was Tricia.

"Dag Girl! Was you even gonna call me back?"

"Yes. I was just getting ready to call you. I had to get myself together first. I just got home from work a couple of hours ago."

"A couple of hours ago?" Tricia asked. "I thought you got off at 5:00."

"I do, but I did some overtime."

"Girl, you sure do work hard. Anyway, I was calling to see what you was up to this weekend."

"I really didn't have any plans. Why? What are you doing?"

"I wanna go to a club or something. Go get some drinks."

"Now, Tricia. You know I don't like clubs. It's too crowded in there."

"Huh? Hello! That's what it's supposed to be: Crowded, Jas! I wouldn't wanna go if it's not. That would be whack!"

"I don't know, Tricia. Me and clubs don't get along. And I know I wasn't that exciting to be with the last time we went to that club."

"You was okay. All the guys that came up to you thought you was a lesbian or something 'cause you turned them all down. And plus, you stuck next to me the whole time when I wasn't dancing."

"Yuk! Eww! A lesbian? They really thought that?"

"Yep. They was asking me what was up with you. But don't mind them. They was just surprised 'cause they thought they had it going on with all their money and that you would just jump to whatever they asked like so many other hoochie chicks."

"Like you?" Jasmine laughed.

"Later for you, girl. I'm just out to have fun. Well maybe just a little bit of their dough," Tricia laughed back. "So anyway, if you wanna go and if you change your mind, just call me. Okay?"

"Okay, I will," Jasmine answered.

"Later, girlfriend!"

"Okay, later," Jasmine said.

Tricia was a cool friend to have, Jasmine thought. They really didn't have all that much in common. They had met in college and had been friends ever since. So Tricia was mainly her only friend. Besides her grandparents, Jasmine had nobody else. Her mother and father both had been killed in a car accident. It had been a terrible blow for Jasmine to handle, for she had adored her mother and father. They were everything to her.

Born in Atlanta, Georgia, she knew nothing but love stemming from a beautiful relationship that her father and mother had. She saw nothing but happiness on their faces. They had shown her that same love that they both harbored. She was happy and excited when she was graduating from public school because she knew that her parents would be proud of her. So proud and happy that she wrote a poem, "Oh How I Love My Mommy and Daddy" and she would read it at the ceremony. But her happiness came to a full stop when her teacher had pulled her away from the ceremony and told her that her mother and father had been killed in a car accident. She would never get a chance to read her poem.

Either I must be real hungry or this Chinese food is real good, Jasmine thought to herself. Eating and looking through the paper, she came across a section where she saw:

New Poet's Lounge
Downtown Brooklyn
Tonight and Tomorrow ~ FREE!
So come hear some poetry and fill your soul

22

Should I go? I'm not doing anything else tonight. I don't wanna go to a club, so I might as well go and enjoy some poetry and see what the new lounge is about. Yep! That's what I'm gonna do. Besides, I have a new outfit that I haven't worn yet. So, I'll wear that tonight. New outfit, new poet's lounge. Yep! Sounds like a plan. I'm gonna go check out this Lyric Luv.

❊   ❊   ❊

WHAT AM I gonna do tonight? It's always the same old weekend. Nothing new happening nowhere. I'm tired of going to clubs. That's getting' played out. Whether it's strip clubs or regular clubs. Both are getting boring. Both have the same old chickenheads, and all they want is money. So why bother?

Daddy was driving downtown Brooklyn when he spotted a new place called Lyric Luv. He rode up to it to see what it was about. It was a place where people go to hear poetry.

Hmm. This sounds like something interesting, although I have never been to nothing like this. It doesn't open up until 10 pm, and it's only 8:30. So, I'll come back. I have nothing else to do, so why not check this place out? Who knows, I might get some new ideas.

Daddy had done a little songwriting and he wondered if poetry was like that. Although he had never been to a poetry reading, he wondered if he would like it. Well, if he didn't like the poetry itself, he certainly would like the surprise that he would see there tonight. And that in itself would make him come back again and again and again.

The Lyric Luv Café on its opening night had a nice turnout. Maybe it was because the hip/hop artist/actor was there. Or maybe people just liked poetry that much. Whatever the reason, the Lyric Luv Café looked like it was gonna have good business in Brooklyn.

This is nice, Jasmine said to herself. She looked radiant with her haircut in a Halle Berry style wearing her new outfit. She was definitely attractive and with her style of dress you would think that she was one who would be up on stage tonight.

"Welcome to the Lyric Luv Café, Miss. I hope you enjoy your night," one of the new members of the new club greeted her as she walked in.

"Thank you! It looks like I will." Jasmine sat down at one of the empty tables. She was looking around and admiring the place. *Wow! This place is really beautiful. Whoever decorated this place sure knew what they were doing.*

The tables were decorated nicely with lighted candles. Even the floors were lit up with assorted colors. *Yea! They really did a number on this place.*

Latief walked out on stage and the crowd went crazy.

What's up everybody! Yea, Yea, Yea!

Welcome to the new Lyric Luv Café.

Where all the poets can have their say.

Where the ears will hear poetry words

Well put together for the soul to yearn.

Do enjoy your evening, listen and admire

These new profound poets whose lyrics are on fire!

The crowd awed and applauded Latief's opening lines and anticipated the newcomers of the spoken word.

Daddy was dressed already for any event. Besides, he didn't want to go home and change, afraid that he would just argue with

"Miss Stress You Out". So why spoil his night by going home to change? What he had on was alright.

There might be some fine sistas there, Daddy said to himself. *I should call Peanuts and see if he wants to go. Naw, that nigga would just put something like this down. I don't mind going by myself. I'll stop in home for a few and if there ain't nothin' poppin off, I'll bounce.*

The atmosphere of the café lounge was new indeed, especially for Daddy because he had never been to a place like this before. The setting was different from the hip-hop clubs he had been to. Jazz music was playing quietly through the surround sound. And he saw a different kind of people. He was used to the fast-paced, hip hop slick kind of crowd. Instead, he witnessed here a more laid back crowd who looked like they were about to enjoy themselves. He said to himself that maybe he should have gone home to change.

The timberland and jeans outfit he had on didn't fit in this type of scene as he had thought. *"Oh Well. I'm here now!"*

Latief had just gotten off the stage when he walked in.

"Damn!" Daddy said. "That was Latief. They got him up in the spot. Yea! This place is bangin'! He's the shit!"

Daddy sat down and admired the scene a little more. And looking around the place he wanted to see if he recognized anybody he knew. He didn't see anybody he knew off hand. But in the far left corner, he thought he recognized somebody. Maybe it was his imagination. Maybe she just stood out because of the spankin' outfit that she had on. Or maybe 'cause she was so damn beautiful.

Wait a minute, that can't be her. Is it? Daddy thought to himself.

It was hard to tell for sure because he was looking at her from the side, plus it was a tad bit dark. But the lighting from the floor and the candlelit tables had given her away. Not to mention her

Halle Berry hairstyle. The waitress had brought her a drink over. She smiled and said thank you. He knew then that was her.

He wanted to go over there, but he didn't quite know how to approach her. Sure, he had no problem when it came to a chick that really didn't mean much. He would just spit out his game and he would have her, simple as that. But she was of another breed. Different. Far from a chickenhead, the regular old girl from the hood. No, Jasmine was more sophisticated, more like a church girl. That's why he didn't know how to come at her. He didn't want to mess up. It was killing him that she was sitting in clear view of him and he couldn't find the nerve to go over and at least speak.

"Fuck it!" he said. "My name is Daddy."

So he put on his coat of confidence, and headed toward her. As soon as he had gotten the nerve and was close to getting out of his seat, some lame ass dude with a tight ass turtleneck on that looked like it made him gasp for air every second, walked up to her and sat in the chair next to her. She had smiled like she knew him, but the turtle-necked brother was making it hard for them to know each other.

Fuck! Daddy said to himself.

Just because one of the poets said that he saw some ladies that were single in the audience didn't mean he had to hop his thirsty ass to her table. And the way she was leaning back, was like she was frightened that he had a nuclear bomb in his mouth.

"Fuck it!" he said again. "I'm gonna go over and help her out." Daddy confidently strolled over to where they was sitting.

"Hey Jazz. Sorry I'm late."

"Hey," Jasmine said back.

"You two together?" the turtleneck dude asked.

"Yea, my man."

"Sorry, I was just keeping her company." He walked off saying, "Shit!" to himself.

"That was smooth, Mr. Singer."

"What?"

"The way you walked over here and saved me from the brother who I thought had a bomb in his mouth!"

They both laughed. They looked at each other for a moment. Jasmine was the first to speak.

"So how are you doing?" she asked.

"I'm good. This place is nice. They really did a nice job hookin' it up. It's hard to tell it was a movie theatre before."

"Is that what it was? I didn't know."

"Yea! Me and my friends used to come here a lot back in the day."

"So, I see you like poetry."

"It's cool," Daddy replied. "I've never really been to something like this before. So are you enjoying yourself?" He looked at her with intense eyes.

"Yes, I am."

"Wait a sec. I just met you this morning on a professional level and now here we are being social."

"Is something wrong with that, Mr. Singer?"

"No not at all, but I'm surprised that you remember me."

"I usually don't forget a kept face."

And how could she forget him? She had just seen him that morning and was thinking about him for most of the day – him and that voice of his. She had seen him when he had walked in the door when she was sitting at her table and had instantly recognized him, and out of the corner of her eye she had seen him notice her at the table. She had wondered if he remembered her.

Apparently, he did because he kept looking in her direction. But

27

the brother who thought that he could mack, came over and interrupted the chemistry that was flowing back and forth between them. They were playing a game. *Did she notice me?* Or *I wonder, did he recognize my game?* Now they were sitting next to each other. Both thinkin' pretty much the same things. Both were attracted to each other. And to both of them, it was brand new.

It was new to Jasmine because she wanted someone in her life, but was still afraid to break out of her cocoon.

It was new for Daddy because he wasn't used to running his mack game down on some chick. But here again, Jasmine was no chick. She had class, and she respected herself. And she had a certain awe about her that Daddy found intriguing.

"I see that you didn't call."

"I was gonna' call tomorrow. I thought that you might have been busy, so I wanted to wait.

"Well, I already ran my mouth about you. I told my people that I heard someone who could really sing."

"Yea? What did they say?"

"Well, usually when I tell them that I heard someone who can sing, they believe me. So they would like to hear for themselves."

"Word!" Daddy said. "So you have good influence on people?"

"I guess," she answered.

"This is ironic or fate. We just met this morning and now we are facing each other, sitting here listening to poetry. It truly is a small world."

"It sure is," she said.

"Do you drink?" Daddy asked her.

"Only Virgin Pina Zula."

"So you want one?"

"Sure. Why not?"

He ordered two; one for her and one for him. He proposed a

toast to him meeting her people and them liking him. And then he proposed a toast to their friendship. They sipped on their drinks and talked some more.

"Well, they are getting ready to end this session tonight. Do you have a lift home?"

"Yes! We Can Get You There car service. Does that sound familiar?"

"Sure does. I work for them!" They both laughed.

"Naw. If you want, I could take you."

"No, that's okay. I don't want to take you out of your way."

"It's no bother! You sure?"

"Yea. I'm sure. I already got arrangements. A car should be outside waiting for me, but thank you anyway."

"No problem, Jasmine."

"You know something? I don't even know your name, Mr. Singer."

"Daddy. I mean Michael. Michael Flowers. That's my name."

"Cute name. Hmm Michael Flowers. Well, Mr. Flowers. Make sure you call me this week coming up. You still have my number, don't you?"

"Yep! I got it."

"Good. Don't forget to call, once again."

He walked her to the car, opened the door for her, and saw the car drive off. He said to himself standing there, *Wow! What a woman!*

THREE

DADDY WAS feeling good about himself. He was in heaven. And not even Cindy could steal him away from that with her nasty attitude. No, not even Cindy. See, Jasmine had to be different, because Daddy never told any girl that he was trying to get his full name like that. He was Daddy to all of them.

"Damn! That girl got a hold on me already," he said.

"I gave up the game, I told her my real name." He smiled. "Wow!"

He walked in his house and Bam! There she was. Cindy. Watching her favorite movie, "Waiting to Exhale."

I can't wait for her ass to exhale her behind out my house! Daddy thought.

"Why are you looking so damn happy?" Cindy asked.

"Why I can't be happy?"

"Well, I wish you would make me happy and get me my fur coat."

"Cindy, please don't start."

"Daddy, why you acting like that?"

"Oh – Now I'm Daddy again."

She got up, went towards him and threw her arms around him.

"You know I love you, baby. It's just that all my friends got one and I don't. Don't you love me? Don't you want me to look nice?"

"Yes I do and yes I do, but I can't spare no fur coat money. I'm trying to stack my bread up. Not spend it as soon as I get it. That's how I hustle now."

She sucked her teeth. "Forget you. You are just so fuckin' cheap. Why can't you hustle full time like Peanuts instead of driving that taxi for no money?"

"See, there you go. Trying to put me on the block 24/7. You somethin' else girl. You know that? Why can't you be a good backbone and support me like you suppose to?"

"You know I got your back."

"No, I don't know that. It's hard to tell."

"Tell me a time when I ain't never had your back."

"Singing! I like singing. I wanna go and record some of my stuff."

"Oh boy! Here we go again with that."

"See what I mean? No support in that area."

"Okay. Okay. Okay. Look. You can sing. You have a nice voice. But Daddy, think for a second. You actually think that you can make it in the music business? It's hard out there for a pimp, so you know it's hard out there for a hustler and that's what you are. And you're good at that."

"Thanks a lot for seeing my potential in negative shit. That really pumps me up."

"Well, it's true. I've seen you flip that dough. Better and faster than I flip pancakes."

No matter how much Daddy wanted to argue with her about that, she was beginning to sound right. Realistically, she was making

31

some sense.

I have in my heyday made some good money. Doing what I do.

Cindy broke his thoughts, sounding more convincing and persuasive.

"And I am your backbone, Daddy, baby. Just look at the times when I hold you down, carrying your work for you. Sometimes picking your stuff up and dropping off. I'm what they call a hustler's girl." She had whispered that in his ear, knowing that would send sexual vibes up and down his spine.

"And you know as well as I do, a hustler's girl gotta' play her role and look good playing her role."

He felt her breasts pressed against his back, just like he felt something creeping down his leg. It was JoJo (his penis) getting hard, responding to the seduction that Cindy was playing on him. Now she knew Daddy, but she knew JoJo a little better. Well enough to know that he would give in to her whispering magic. Daddy cursed his dick for betraying him like that. Suppose he didn't want to have sex with this broad tonight?

Well if he didn't, it was too late. Cindy had won JoJo over, which was pretty much the case all the time.

"Alright, Cindy. Okay! Suppose I said I'll think about getting you the fur coat. Would that ease your mind?"

"Yes. That would ease my mind. Just like the thang thang I'm holding in my hand would please my behind."

She was massaging his shit like she was the one who thought the whole Karma Sutra thing up. Daddy was so weak in his legs, he couldn't take it.

"Can we go lay down?" he asked, as if he was the student asking the teacher for permission.

But Cindy said no, and told him to put his hands on the wall, like he was under arrest or something. She stripped him down to his bare skin, but only down to his jeans and boxers. She left his top clothes on. Caressing his nipples and still whispering magic in his ears.

Daddy was no fuckin good. He was lost somewhere. Here he was, this strong ass nigga', but under her spell, he was a weak ass bitch.

Wow! Talk about As The World Turns! Cindy moved her tongue up and down Daddy's buttocks until she saw what she'd been looking for. It was JoJo peeking from the other side. She gladly went around with both palms on his ass and took his chocolate bar in her mouth and sent Daddy to heaven. She was doing what she did best. Giving pleasure.

When Daddy was almost close to cummin', she stopped. She got up and whispered in his ear, "I want that thang thang inside me while I'm on all fours. "

She pulled him to the bed, walked on it like she was a bitch in heat, grabbed his dick and put it in her and that was it. It was like he was a pirate and he had found a treasure. He was stroking and stroking and stroking. And she was pushing and pushing and pushing.

"Daddy! I'm about to cum!"

"Me too!" Daddy cried.

"Daddy, I'm cummin'. I'm cummin'! Shit, shit shit!"

They both came at the same time.

"Wow! That was fuckin good, girl! Damn! Where you be learnin' shit like that?"

"It just comes natural. Why, did you enjoy it?"

"Did I enjoy it? Shit. I'm so out of it, I couldn't even get up if one of my customers was calling me. All I wanna' do is just lay here. Can't even get up and take a shower."

Cindy said, "Don't. Just lay here and go to sleep."

She got up and went to the bathroom, came back with a warm

rag and wiped his shit off. Damn! Even that felt good.

"Man, you sure want that fur coat, don't you?"

"Yep, sure do. But that's not why I'm doing this."

"Yea, yea, yea! Anyway, I'll still think about it. Let me sleep on it." And with that being said, Daddy was fast asleep.

When Daddy was out of it, Cindy would always sneak in his clothes and take a few dollars. This time, she wanted a little more, just in case he didn't decide to get her that coat. She was going to get it one way or another. She knew he carried at least $1000 in his pocket every day. When he came in here, he didn't have a chance to put it up, 'cause she had jumped on him as soon as he came in.

So she dug through his clothes, took a couple of hundred dollars and found a card with some girl's name, Jasmine Greene on it. It was a business card, but why did it have on the back, "You have a nice voice. If I can help you, call me!"

"Bitch!" Cindy said. "Like hell you gonna' help him." She ripped the card up and threw it in the garbage.

Well the weekend was over and it was back to work for those who did work. Daddy was thrilled 'cause he thought he would get that beautiful passenger again. It was unlikely though to get the same passenger twice. Still, that shouldn't stop him from hoping, right?

He could not stop thinking about Friday that had just passed. It was a Good Friday. He had met a beautiful girl while at work. Then that same night at this new café lounge called "The Lyric Luv," he had bumped into her. They had talked and gotten to know each other a little better. So why wouldn't he, early on this Monday morning, hope to run into her again.

"I'm going to call her today," Daddy said to himself. He had reached in his pocket just to see if he still had the card, but it wasn't there.

34

He frowned up his face, "What the...?"

So he started searching all around his pockets, but couldn't find what he was looking for.

Shit! Damn! What the fuck did I do with that card? He thought to himself and tried to remember

His phone rang and interrupted his thoughts. "Hello?"

"Yo. What up, Kid?"

"Oh. What up, Peanuts." Damn.

"What up with you? Why you sound like that?"

"Ain't nothin'." Daddy said.

"Naw, I was just calling you to tell you I was gonna be a little late getting at The Club House this afternoon, that's all."

"Aaight. I'll see you later then." Daddy answered.

FOUR

"YOU STILL think you can take me, huh, kid? Shh. Come on, Peanuts. You know you can't fuck wit me on this court."

"My handle is viscous."

"That might be true, but your game done fell off since high school, while mine's stayed with me."

"So why every time we play I bust that ass?"

"Close game tho."

"I still won."

"You lucky we gotta coach today, or else."

Peanuts said, "Nigga, please! You lucky."

They were still acting like kids, competing against one another. They had been at it since high school. They both were good in school, but Daddy could handle that rock like nobody could. He was the star of his school. All the girls, ALL of them would give him their attention every time he walked by.

And even though he and Peanuts were boys, Peanuts had shown a tad bit of jealousy toward his friend. If it wasn't the coach saying how good he was, it was Daddy's game that spoke for itself. It was remarkable. And even nowadays, the kids looked up to Daddy. And Peanuts even envied that!

"Hey! Daddy!" one of the boys had yelled out.

"What's up, Kareem? How's my little hoopster doing?"

"I'm good. Trying to work on my crossover like yours."

"Gimme a break." Peanuts said. "You think he got a crossover?"

"Awww. Be quiet, Peanuts. You just hatin'. Let me see what you got, Kareem."

"Naw, let me see what you taught this little fellow."

Peanuts jumped in. "Okay, Kareem. Let's see that crossover."

Peanuts didn't know what happened. Either he was getting rusty or the boy was too quick for him, 'cause he put some kind of magic on him that had him and Daddy amazed.

"Damn!" Daddy said. "He shook your ass!"

"He did it when I wasn't ready."

"Yep. Sure you wasn't ready." Daddy laughed. "Face it, Peanuts. You're a bump. Can't even defend a 12-year-old."

"Yea, yea, yea. So what, he got lucky."

"Lucky my ass. You damn near twisted your ankle. See if you wouldn't have jumped out there you wouldn't have gotten embarrassed." They both laughed.

"The boy do gotta' mean crossover." Peanuts said.

Daddy and Peanuts finished up their coaching stuff with the kids and started packing up to leave. A voice yelled out Daddy's name. It was Kareem.

"What's up, Kareem?" Daddy asked.

"Are you still gonna' get the team uniforms so we can look like a real team?"

"Of course I am, Champ!" Daddy replied. "They are already getting made. They should be done next week."

"Cool!" the young boy happily said. "You sure are a good person. You treat us good. I wish I had a father like you."

And after saying that, he ran back towards the other boys.

After Kareem had penetrated Daddy's heart with those words, all he could do was just stand there and feel the warmth of those words coming from that boy. Daddy knew that Kareem's father was not in his life due to a Life bid in upstate New York. So it was typical for a kid that young to look at him like a role model.

It was amazing what he did with them: Coaching them in basketball, teaching them things about life. He talked to them when he saw something was wrong. He was there for those kids in every way possible. But for Kareem to say something like that, it was brand new to Daddy. His mother had already told him that she wanted a grandchild. But in his life to today, he had nobody to go have a baby with.

Certainly not Cindy. For God's sake, not Cindy.

"Yo! Daddy! Yo! Damn, Nigga'! Where you at," Peanuts said. "You in a daze or something?"

"Oh! My bad, man! I was just caught up in thought."

"You sure was. Let's get outta here kid. You ready?"

"Yea. I'm ready."

They started out the front door and when they got outside, they saw Hustle Jack in front of his van doing what he does best, hustling his clothes, chanting his favorite line: "My name is Hustle Jack. I got this and I got that. From girls to ladies gear, from boys to men's wear. If I don't got it, the stores don't have it either. And if they do my prices are much cheaper."

Daddy and Peanuts both were laughing at his rhymes as they walked up to his van to have a look.

"What you got Hustle Jack?" Daddy asked.

"I got these New Religion jeans and Timbs for you my brother."

"Naw," Daddy said. "I got enough jeans."

But what he saw in the far left corner raised his interest. "What kind of coat is that?" he asked.

"Oh! That's fox fur."

"Word! How much is that?"

"Well, they cost about $600 in the store, but I'll let it go for $350 for you."

"Let me see it."

"Sure," Hustle Jack said.

"What you think about this, Peanuts?" Daddy asked.

"Looks good. Who you getting it for?"

"Cindy, who else?"

"I thought you would say that. You know that girl wants a mink. And that's fox fur."

"She won't know the difference."

"I don't know kid. When it comes to clothes, bitches know."

"Well, she just gonna' have to like this. Fuck it. Give me that. I got $300 right now."

"It's yours," Hustle Jack said, "And trust me, my brother. She's gonna' love you for this."

"You know Cindy is gonna trip," Peanuts said. "She wants a mink and you bought her a fox. Big difference."

"What you talkin' about man? This is a nice coat. And it don't look cheap."

"I'm just saying, Kid. She's gonna' know the difference. And then, there goes another argument."

"Well, I bought it now, so she just gonna' have to accept it, that's all."

"All right! But I bet you are gonna be calling me to tell me that she threw that coat right back at you."

"We'll see, Peanuts. We'll see. "

"Aye yo! Kid, drop me off home. My car is in the shop."

"All right. Hop in."

"Thanks," Peanuts said.

"Aye yo. You sure you don't wanna work with me? 'Cause damn, nigga! You need a new car!"

Daddy looked at Peanuts and said, "I'm sure."

After Daddy had dropped off Peanuts, he headed home thinking about the card he had lost and how he was gonna get in contact with Jasmine. He thought maybe she might be at the Café Lounge this weekend, but that was too far. He wanted to speak to her sooner than that. He wanted to meet her people and see what they thought about his singing. He wanted to hear her voice. But the main want he wanted, was to make love to her.

❀　❀　❀

MICHAEL FLOWERS. What an interesting name, Jasmine thought. And the man that owns that name was interesting. He was not like all the others who had tried to befriend her for whatever reason they had in mind. And it was probably for one thing: Sex. That's what they all wanted, but there was something about this Michael Flowers that warmed to her for he was charming. He reminded her of her father in a way. He had always called her Princess, made her feel like she was of a fairy tale, like the stories he used to read to her. Like she belonged to a prince. So with Michael Flowers being so charming, he fit the description of a prince. She knew she shouldn't think like that, but her fairy tale dreams disallowed her to think otherwise. But yet, she lived in a world that was no fairytale. A world that was full of ugliness. A world that felt so empty.

The doorbell rang and rescued her from her thoughts that she was having.

"Who is it?"

"Girl, it's me. Tricia. Buzz me up!"

"Okay, okay. Gosh is someone after you or something?"

"Yea! Jack Frost! It's so damn cold out there you would have thought they moved Brooklyn to the North Pole! Hold up. I know you're ready to go, right?"

"Yep! All I have to do is slip on something and we out!"

"Girl, what the hell have you been doing? You know we always go get our nails and feet done every Monday. So why you ain't ready?"

"Shut up! It won't take me long. Tricia? This weekend that's coming up. I want you to go with me to this new poetry club. The place is cool."

"Poetry club! Why would I want to go listen to some corny ass poems from some whack ass brothers?"

"Because they're not corny for one, and for two, it'll be something different than clubs all the time."

"At least there is dancing at those clubs. You can't dance at no poetry place."

"Tricia, it's not all about shaking your ass all the time and getting all sweaty. We could go there this weekend and have a nice time."

"Well, is there any rappers there? Up and coming or established?"

"Latief is the host."

"Latief? Awww he's alright. But I mean like Jada Kiss or Naz or somebody like that."

"Sorry. Nope. I don't know, Jasmine. But I'll think about it."

"Good! Let's go get our nails done."

FIVE

"WHAT THE fuck is this?" Cindy shouted.

"A fur coat."

"Okay, then let me ask you another question. Who is supposed to be wearing this?"

"What you mean, who supposed to be wearing it. It's yours."

"Daddy, are you stupid? Or you just don't give a fuck? Which one? Because ain't no way in hell or heaven am I wearing this piece of shit imitation fur. Damn! Why would you go out and buy some crap like this?"

"Listen. I don't see shit wrong with this coat."

"Of course not, 'cause you don't have to wear it. I knew you was cheap, but now I really know. You are one cheap ass bastard."

"Cindy, you are just ungrateful. There ain't nothin' wrong with this coat and you know it."

"Daddy, do you know what you bought. You bought me a bullshit ass fox fur that's gonna' shed after a couple of wears. You probably bought it from off the street corner somewhere and paid nothing for it. And you think I supposed to jump in your arms and say, 'oooh baby. Thank you, thank you so much!'

"Well nigga! No! I don't want this stupid lookin' piece of shit."

"So what I supposed to do with it then?"

"I don't care what you do with it. Give it to your fake church-goin' mother."

"Yo! Watch your fucking mouth about my mother!"

"Oh! Puuul-lease! You know all those people that go to church is so fake and your mother is no exception."

"A yo! Why you gotta be a bitch, Bitch! And talk about her like that? My mother don't bother you. So why you gotta talk about her like that?"

"Pul-lease you know, like I know that your mama don't like me. I could tell. Just because I am who I am she despises me. She probably wish you was hooked up with one of those fake ass church broads instead of me."

"That ain't got nothing to do with you calling my mother out her name. So slow your roll."

"No nigga you need to fast past your role if you still wanna have this. I'm tired Mike. I'm so fed up with you. And I saw him the other day doing good with his brand new Benz."

"So you still seein' that nigga?"

"No but he did ask me out. He wanted me to go to Miami for a weekend with him but Nooooo. I wanna play faithful with your cheap ass. I should have went."

"You think you gonna hurt me if you go wit that nigga huh? Naw! Bitch, you got me fucked up. Go ahead and go to Miami with that bitch ass nigga. I don't care if he took your ass to Canada!"

Cindy burst out laughing. "Oh. Now you wanna be thug and act like you won't miss this pussy. You funny."

"Like I said before. If you wanna bring other niggas into this, there's the door."

"You know something Mike. Maybe I will," and after saying that, Cindy put on her coat, picked up her bag and left out the door.

❀ ❀ ❀

"WORD! GET the fuck outta here."

"Yea, Peanuts. She broke out. We had our usual little argument but this time I guess it must have gotten thick, where as she couldn't take it. So she bounced."

"Dam kid! I told you that coat wasn't gonna be the one. She wanted a mink and you bought her a fox." Peanuts burst out laughing.

"That shit ain't funny. What the hell I spose to do with this coat?"

"Sorry Dawg! But I told you so. That's all I'm saying. Stop being so cheap and shit like that won't happen."

"It's much more than that anyway. Cindy don't give a nigga no support. All she wants is material shit."

"C'mon nigga. What girl don't?"

"True. But she's just berserk with it. She probably wouldn't have wanted one so much if she didn't see Shay-Shay with one."

"Don't blame that shit on me, Dawg. I gets whatever Shay-Shay wants because that's my queen and she deserves it. The way she looks out for me."

"See what I mean tho? She gots your back. That bitch Cindy don't do nothing but beg and gold dig her way through life. She went back to that nigga name "Stacks". I guess he must have got it going on, 'cause she broke right the fuck out when I told her there's the door when she brought him up. I swear boy, bitches ain't shit."

"I hear you, Dawg. But yo! I gotta' make this run. I'll holla at you later."

"Aight Peanuts. I get up wit you later."

After Peanuts drove off, Daddy started to wonder what he was gonna do. He was off today from work, so it was really nothing happening. He drove around Brooklyn enjoying himself because he loved driving. As he drove past that new spot called the Lyric Luv café, he remembered the night that he saw Jasmine there. He thought about her and wondered what she was up to. Wondered if she was at work. Wondered if she would be upset if he just popped up at her job. Wondered why he was already at the Brooklyn Bridge headed in that direction. He just wondered.

❀   ❀   ❀

"HELLO. UMM, I'm looking for someone who works here. She's an editor, her name is Jasmine Greene."

"Yes. And may I ask what business that you have with her?"

"Yes. Umm I have a delivery – these flowers."

"I can sign for them," the receptionist said.

"Look it's very urgent that I give these to her in person. Is there any way possible that I can?"

"No there isn't. It's the company's policy that all deliveries be made on the ground floor. Sorry, no."

Shit, Daddy said to himself. He was getting mad. He didn't drive all the way here just to leave flowers at the receptionist desk. His main intention was seeing Jasmine, not just to drop off flowers and leave.

"So can you call her and tell her to come pick them up herself?"

"Sorry no. We're not allowed to disturb the editors."

"Listen, lady. It's important that I see her today and give her these. "

She cut him off. "Now you listen. I told you that I can't let you up or call her up to come down. So you would just have to make up with her on your own time."

"Make up with her?" Daddy said surprised.

"Yes," said the receptionist. "It's obvious. You keep begging and bugging to let you up to plead your case, so you must be in the doghouse and trying to get out. "

Daddy just shook his head and said, "You must be miserable and jealous that no one is bringing you flowers."

"You call those cheap things flowers?"

Daddy was just about to say something when he heard a familiar voice call out his name.

"Michael?"

"Oh, hey! How you doing, Jasmine?"

"What are you doing here Mr. Singer? You changed your job — you deliver flowers now?"

"Oh, no! These are for you."

"For me? Oh how sweet. They're beautiful. And they match your name, Flowers."

"Yea how 'bout that. They do, don't they?"

"Come on. Come up to my office."

He looked at the receptionist and smiled and stuck out his chest as if to say he had won the battle between them. She rolled her eyes at him.

"What's up with Miss Miserable?"

"Oh don't mind her. That's just the way she is."

"Well, she sure was giving me a hard time to get in touch with you."

"Well she really is not to call up to the floor or send anyone up. You know, it's a security thing. Luckily I went to get me a cappuccino or we would have missed each other."

"Yea that is luck."

"So what brings you to Manhattan today?"

"Oh, I was off today and I had lost your number and I wanted to see you. I had no other way, so I took a chance on coming here. Wow! Is this your office?"

"Yep! This is my second home."

"Well, you got it goin' on, Miss Editor. What does an editor do anyway?"

"Well my job is to make sure articles have some type of taste to be printed in our newspaper."

"And that's it? Then I can write me an article and it might get printed in your newspaper?" He joked.

"It's not that simple," Jasmine said. "You'd be surprised at some of the junk that don't make it. "

"Well my article would make it, cause I's got some tasty stuff to write about."

"I'm sure you do, Mr. Singer."

"Why do you always call me Mr. Singer?"

"Cause it fits you. You sing, so Mr. Singer fits you."

"Okay, so you edit. So Miss Editor fits you." They both laughed.

"So what about these people that you know…that you said would like to hear my voice?"

"Can I ask you something?" She said.

"Sure go ahead."

"Are you ready for the world? 'Cause when my people hear you, they are going to love you. I mean you have a great voice and you have the look also." *Boy does he have the look*, she thought to herself. "So that's why I asked you, are you ready for the world."

"Yea. I'm ready," Daddy said.

SIX

DADDY'S VOICE was incredible. The people who were listening were impressed by the talent that this young man possessed. It was remarkable the way he hit every note at the right time and every song that the man asked him to sing – he smashed it. Daddy himself was excited as well as amazed, because of who he was in front of singing for.

"Wow!" The man said. "Where did you find him at Jazz? This boy here got one helluva voice."

"Told you," she said.

Daddy, so surprised said, "You're Eddie Tate! I mean the real Eddie Tate?"

Everybody laughed.

"Man I love your radio show. Mr. Tate, you're hot."

"Thank you, son, but that voice you got is crazy, off the chain. I know some people that know some people that would love to sign you right up."

"For real?" Daddy burst out like he was a little boy that couldn't contain himself.

"Yep, for real. By the way what do they call you? "

"Oh, Daddy! They call me Daddy, but my real name is Michael Flowers."

"Daddy, huh. Where'd you get that name?"

"It's just a nickname I picked up from my hood. You can call me Mike though. "

"Naw, it's cool kid, cause with a voice like that, hell I'll call you Daddy. Just hold on a sec. Let me go make some calls. Be right back."

"Okay," Daddy said. "A yo Jasmine. I didn't know you knew him! Eddie Tate, wow!"

"Yep! I know him and other people, too."

"I've met a lot of people doing what I do."

"I told you they would love your voice, and I knew that you would be getting signed almost immediately."

"Damn! I feel like I'm flying right now."

Eddie Tate came back with a big ass smile on his face.

"Son, some people at Def Jam want to meet you right away. Are you busy today?"

"Naw, I'm not busy at all."

"Okay, here's what you need to do, and ask for this person. He's expecting you. "

"Def Jam, wow! It feels like I hit the lottery or something."

"You have son, you have! Jasmine, it's like you pulled a gift from out the sky with this one. Thank you, dear."

"No problem, Steve. I'll call you next week."

He kissed her on the cheek and shook Daddy's hand. And they both left out. When they got outside, Daddy kissed and hugged her so much, you would have thought that he had found a new love. Which he did.

"Wow, Daddy! You sure are excited."

"Oh my bad, I ..."

"No, it's okay. You should be overwhelmed. You're about to hit it big."

Surprised to hear someone like Jasmine call him Daddy, he said, "That's just an old hood name that they call me."

"No, it's okay. I think it's cute. I like it."

He looked into her eyes and was so transfixed by her warmth and smile that he just leaned over and kissed her passionately. He quickly pulled away and said, "I'm sorry. I got carried away."

"It's ok. You can do that again," Jasmine said.

SEVEN

THE PEOPLE at Def Jam were more than impressed with Daddy's voice. They were excited, for it had been a long time since someone walked into their studio with such talent like his. They had produced successful R&B singing in their time, but Daddy was different. He had soul, as well as the looks. Every song that they asked him to sing, he took them somewhere, as if they were riding on the waves of his voice. No doubt, a recording artist was in the making.

"Can I have your autograph?" Jasmine teased.

"See there you go having jokes," Daddy smiled.

"Well that's what's going to happen. I could see you now writing your name all over the place."

"This whole thing is brand new to me," Daddy said. "I still can't believe it's happening."

"Believe it, Booboo. They want you and now you are gonna be a hit."

Daddy could not contain the big ass smile on his face.

"Just a week ago you were a passenger, now you're in the passenger seat."

"How 'bout that!" Jasmine said. "You have a nice car."

"You think so?" Daddy said surprised.

"Yea, I like it. Not everybody has to have a Benz or a BMW, even though they're nice. It doesn't make a difference to me. I can't drive."

"Are you serious?" he said.

"Yep, I can't drive."

"Oww. It's easy once you get the hang of it. I'll teach you."

"With the busy schedule you gonna be having I doubt you're going to have time, but that would be kool."

"I'll make time for you."

"Oww, how sweet."

"Naw, I'm serious. It's because of you I'll be busy anyway, so why can't I take time to do you a favor and teach you how to drive? Besides, I would like to see you more."

There was silence between them after he had said that, until she broke it.

"Do you know that you just passed my building?"

"Yep! I'm taking you to dinner if I can, if you don't mind. I feel like celebrating."

"Now how did you know that I didn't have anything planned?"

"I didn't. I just took a guess that's all."

"Well, I am a little hungry, so I guess I'm yours."

❀   ❀   ❀

THE KID Kat Klub was always popping on the weekends. Every hustler and businessmen alike were there to bring up its already growing popularity. Out of almost fifty strippers, ten were a sight for sore eyes to see. And Cindy was one of those ten. She was seductive and alluring...the way she moved her bangin' body around that pole would capture the attention of both men and women. Her stage name was Pussycat. And when PussyKat came out to perform, everyone wanted to see. It was like watching a ballerina girl do her thing, but only on a pole. The magic came through from her eyes. When she looked at you, you were hers and she had you stuck. That was what got Daddy ... her eyes.

"What's up PussyKat," Stacks said.

"Hey Baby. Did you like my show?" Cindy asked.

"Of course I did. So did everybody else, I see."

❀   ❀   ❀

When Daddy met Cindy

"DAMN! SHAY-SHAY! Who is that nigga with Peanuts?" Cindy asked. "He is fine as hell."

"Oh that's Daddy, him and Nuts are boys. They grew up together."

"Why you feeling him or something, want me to put in a good word for you?"

"Naw girl, I got this, I saw that I had his attention when I was on stage. So I'mma go over there and give him a Pussykat lap dance. And he will be under my spell from there."

"I hear you talking, bitch. Go do your thang," Shay-Shay said.

Cindy wasn't lying either. She knew that lap dance would do it. It worked every time. Although, she did think Daddy was cute, her main motive was money. She knew that Peanuts was paid. And if Daddy was hanging out with him, he also had cheddar. She was hungry for those type of niggas who busted for a living. And she had every right to, being that she grew up around it. Her mother and aunts had their share of men who were street hustlers, and she saw how their lifestyles of glitter and gold was very attractive. It was easy to follow suit. So her way of life was strictly materialistic.

"A yo! Peanuts. Why is that girl staring at me with those sexy ass eyes while she is talking to your girl Shay-shay?"

"I don't know kid. Why don't you ask her cause they on their way over here right now."

"Can I give you a lap dance?"

And before Daddy could answer anything, Pussykat was in his lap doing what she does best.

Daddy asked her, "So is this why they call you Pussykat?"

"I guess. I don't know. Why? You like the way Pussykat feel in your lap?"

"Pussykat feels damn good in my lap. You know how to do this shit for real, Ma."

"I aim to please," Cindy said in a seductive tone.

"I tell you what, Ma. Why don't I buy you a drink and we talk some shit. 'Cause you rubbing up and down in my lap ain't cutting it."

"What's the matter? You can't take it?"

Daddy took a fifty dollar bill out, put it in the string of PussyKat's thong and whispered in her ear. "Naw, I can't take it, if you keep rubbing up against me I'mma want some of this right here and now."

Cindy smiled, got up off his lap knowing that she had him right where she wanted him.

"So PussyKat, do you like what you do?" Daddy asked.

"I mean, it's okay. It gets me a little money here and there."

"It sure seems like you be into what you do."

"Hey! If you gonna do it, might as well do it good, right?"

"And Mama you sure do it good," Daddy said.

Smiling, Pussykat asked, "So did you enjoy the show?"

"Fuck yea. I enjoyed the show. I see that you are very popular up in here. Everyone wanna see you dance."

"Yep! It's cool knowing that you can have an audience so focused on what you're doing on stage. Even if it's like doing it on stage. Even if it is dirty dancing."

"I know that's right," Daddy said. "So what up now, Ma?"

"What you mean?"

"I'm saying what we gonna do now? I mean here we are talking and drinking. We might as well hook up."

"I don't even know your name. And besides, what kind of girl you think I am anyway?"

"My bad, ma. They call me Daddy, and I think you're the kind of girl that likes to have fun and we can do that together."

"Daddy, huh?"

"Yep that's my street name."

"Well I would hope so, cause I can't see your mama naming you Daddy."

They both laughed.

"Yea, I can see we gonna have fun," Daddy exclaimed.

It was like they were made for each other. Neither could keep their hands off the other. Cindy gave Daddy that Pussykat ass that he was thirsty for. And Daddy licked her into an oblivion. But things were moving too fast. Cindy had shared an apartment with her long-time friend Tricia, but nowadays spent most of her time over at Daddy's. She even had her own drawer.

"Damn Daddy. You eat pussy better than anybody I fuckin now. I can't stop shaking or cummin'. Shit!"

"So you like it.?"

"Like it? I used to be sane. Now you got me going crazy and shit. Fuck yes, I like. Keep going."

Cindy woke up out of her sleep after last night's good ass sexin' that Daddy gave her to surprise a breakfast in bed. The scent of bacon woke her up.

"Wake up sleepyhead, time to eat."

"Mmm, this smells good. Wow! All this!"

"Well, I didn't know if you like strawberries so I made plain pancakes and strawberry pancakes, scrambled eggs with cheese of course, bacon, cereal and orange strawberry juice."

"You mean to tell me a street nigga like you can cook?"

"I watched my mother cook while I was growing up, so yea. I'm good in the kitchen, as well as in the bedroom."

"Modest too, huh? But I think I like your cooking better."

"Yea, ok smarty."

"Naw, I'm just kiddin' on that one. Shit. The way you put me to sleep last night, your cooking can't come close, even though this shit tastes good as hell. Damn I'm at IHOP."

After they ate breakfast, Daddy took Cindy shopping at the Green Acres Shopping Mall in Queens. Cindy was like a little girl at Chuck E. Cheese's. Hell, the way this morning was going, she thought it was her birthday. In fact, she thought it was every holiday on the calendar including St. Patrick's Day, which is associated with the color of green.

And that color was what she saw when Daddy pulled out a stack of 100 dollar bills and chipped off a nice corner of it and handed it to her and said, "Do you, Ma."

Cindy surprised that he did this, took the little corner of bills, which she was not used to. Other niggas who took her shopping before just paid for what she picked out.

"Damn, nigga! What you trying to do, spoil me rotten?"

"Na, ma. That ain't it. I just like to look out for people I fuck wit."

57

"Well if you keep going on like this, a girl could get used to this."

"We good, ma."

And with that being said, Cindy went to do her thang. She bought all the designer stuff, Dolce & Gabana, Timberland boots, Sammy Choo's, Rocawear, perfume, everything that appealed to her went into shopping bags. She was having the time of her life. She had had guys spend money on her before, but this here was it. Daddy wasn't cheap and he himself had taste and liked to dress.

"I see you like Rocawear too huh?" Cindy said.

"No doubt, this is my shit here. It's all I really wear. I see you been having fun tho."

"Yep. Shopping is always fun."

"I bet it is. I bet it is."

"So what do we do now, Daddy?"

"I don't know, I was thinking about going to Paris."

"Paris?"

"Yea, ain't you hungry by now with all this shopping?"

"Yea, but why all the way to Paris?"

"It's only in Manhattan."

"Manhattan?"

"Yea they got a restaurant called Paris. The food is slammin'."

"Embarrassing, I swore you was talking about Paris, Paris."

Daddy started laughing out loud. "Naw, Ma. I wasn't talking about the city Paris, even tho' we could go one day."

"You got me on that one. You got me," Cindy chuckled. "Yea, let's go to Paris, the restaurant. I am kind of hungry."

So they hopped in Daddy's Honda Accord and drove off.

"So how long have you been working at the Kid Kat Klub?"

"For a year. On and off tho'."

"Why on and off?"

"Gosh, what am I, in an interview or something?"

"Naw, ma. I'm just kickin' it, that's all."

"Well if you must know, I was just getting tired of stripping. At times, I felt like I wanted to do something else with my life. Then when I'm on that stage, it seems like this is the only thing I'm good at."

"So you like dancing?"

"Yea, I mean dancing gives me freedom, when I'm half naked in front of people and dancing all over the place like that, I'm free to be me."

"You don't be nervous?"

"When I first started, yea. But now it's a breeze."

"So what is the something else that you might wanna do?"

"I always wanted to dance, not stripping, but dancing on videos. That's like my dream."

"Word! So what's up?"

"What you mean what's up?"

"Why don't you go for it? You already got some good moves."

"Boy, please. Don't you know you have to have some connections? It's not what you know. It's who you know."

"You got a point there. But sometimes going for what you know, you just might bump into the right person."

❀   ❀   ❀

DADDY SAT in his apartment in heavy thought, soaking up all the events that just took place a few days ago. Brand new things were happening in his life and he was excited. He couldn't decide on which was more exciting, having a record deal or being with Jasmine. Of course, he could have his pick of any girl he wanted once his music career took off. But Jasmine was a different story.

For every time she looked into his eyes, she stole a piece of his heart. And boy did he enjoy being with her. For every moment that they were together, he felt free. No pressure, no stress, just bliss. His thoughts switched to a different channel when his eyes fell on the belongings of Cindy. She had left most of her stuff there and he hadn't heard from her since she broke out. He wondered if he would ever hear from her. Not that he was thrilled by the idea. It's just that he wanted no problems. Things were going good for him with Jasmine and he didn't need Cindy's bullshit. But truth be told, people sometimes get what they don't want.

❀ ❀ ❀

"DAMN! CINDY, that rock is big ass shit! When did you get that?"

"I just got it yesterday while we were in Miami," Cindy said with a big ass smile on her face. "You like it?"

"Like it? I love it! That nigga must've got pussy whipped down there, huh?"

"Well, yea. And also he said he didn't wanna chance us being apart no more. You know, me and Stacks was together for two years before we broke up."

"So you gonna marry dat nigga huh?" Shay-Shay asked.

"This is just an engagement ring. That nigga just threw it on my hand without even saying anything 'bout marriage. You know how hustlers are. Tying the knot is the last thing on their minds."

"What about Daddy?"

"What about him? Shit! Fuck that cheap ass nigga. He can go to hell, for all I care. You should have seen that poor excuse for a fur coat he bought me. I wanted to slap fire out his ass. He got mad as hell when I told him to give it to his fake church-going mother."

"Girl, stop! You said that?"

"Yep, sure did. He was burning up. So what? I don't care."

"Here comes my booboo. I'm gonna change. Tell him I'll be right out."

"What up Peanuts."

"'Sup Cindy. Where Shay-Shay at?"

"Oh, she just went inside to change. She'll be right out."

"What up with you though?"

"Shit. I'm chillin'. Still dancin' for dollars."

"So what happened to you and my boy?"

"Oh, he didn't tell you?"

"He told me you left him for that nigga Stacks."

"No. I left his cheap ass because he don't give a hell how I look or feel. He's corny and he living in the past with a beat up old ass Honda. That's why I broke out."

"I told him that he should open up a little and come hustle with me and get some real money."

"He don't wanna do that Peanuts. No, he'd rather drive that damn cab, making no money and dream about singing."

"Yea, that do sound whack."

"Because he's whack, Peanuts. Anyway, enough about him. I see you and my girl still hangin' in there."

"Yea. We kool...Aye yo. What the fuck is that on your finger?"

"Oh this?" Cindy held her hand up so that Peanuts could get a real good look at it, hoping he would run and tell Daddy, which he would.

"Stacks gave it to me. This shit is hot, ain't it?"

"Oh, so you engaged now? Damn you move fast."

"This ring ain't nothin' but an attachment for me to get bigger end shit, like a Benz."

"I hear that hot shit."

"Peanuts, can I ask you a question?"

Before Cindy could ask him, Shay-Shay came out.

"Hey Suga Luv," she said to Peanuts. "I'm ready baby. Can you drop Cindy off at her mom's?"

"Yea. I gotta take care of something in that area anyway."

"Ok then, drop me off first and drop her at her mom's; then take care of your business and I'll be getting dinner ready."

"Alright Boo."

"I see my girl be taking care of you huh? Getting dinner ready for her Boo."

"Yea she's good with stuff like that."

"This Benz is hard as hell. The streets is being real good to you huh?"

"I mean, it's what I do, Cin. I gotta get that bread. I gotta look good. You know what I'm sayin'?"

"I hear you, my nigga. So Peanuts, when are we gonna fuck again?"

He knew that was coming, that's why his hands was sweaty. Every time he was with Cindy alone something happened between them. And he knew she wanted him and he her. She was sexy as shit, and she knew how to throw that kitty kat at him.

"There you go, you a sex freak!"

"I know, but you like it, don't you?"

"Shit yea!" he exclaimed. "But what about your home girl? You don't have no conscious on that, like feeling guilty?"

"The only thing I'm feeling right now is horny."

And with saying that she leaned over to him and started massaging his shit. She unzipped his Rocawear jeans and pulled out his shit and started sucking on it while Peanuts was driving.

"Damn! You my kind of bitch!"

"And you my kind of nigga! You should have been mine. I always wanted you. And I know you wanted me."

"You damn right I wanted you. Daddy didn't know what he was doing or had."

She kept sucking on him until he came all in her mouth and he damn near crashed. Cindy leaned back up and smiled knowing that she had claimed another victim, knowing that she had Peanuts under her sexual spell.

❀ ·❀   ❀

THE BOYS Club was having its first basketball game. Daddy's young squad, the Turfs, was playing another young team named the Ballers and everybody came to see these young kids play ball and have fun. Daddy had brought along Jasmine to meet his boy Peanuts and of course to show Jasmine what he liked doing with these kids. Peanuts had already been there at the club, coaching the boys on a few moves before the game started. When Daddy walked in with Jasmine, Peanuts looked like he was struck by lightning.

"What's up, Peanuts? What's up Turfs?"

All the boys said, "What's up to Daddy," in unison.

"What's good, Daddy? And who is this lovely lady?"

"This is Jasmine. Jasmine, this is my boy, Peanuts. Peanuts this is Jasmine."

"Nice to meet you," Jasmine said to Peanuts, while shaking his hand.

"The pleasure is all mine," he said. "So are you the one that's got my boy's head all in the clouds?"

"No it ain't like that, I don't think. We just cool."

"Cool my butt. This dude always talking about you."

"Is that so?" she blushed.

Daddy jumped in and said, "I thought we was boys and you telling on me like that? Wow!"

63

They all laughed.

The game was under way and the Turfs was looking good, especially Lil Kareem, the boy was a natural.

"Go Kareem!" Daddy shouted.

It was easy. Kareem stole the ball and flew down court and laid it up for two pounds. The Turfs were going to win their first game.

"So what do you think about my little basketball team?"

"I think it's great. You are doing something real good. And the kids seem like they look up to you." "Yea. It's kool. Me and Peanuts love coaching these boys. It gives us something to do while it keeps them out of trouble. Right Peanuts?"

"Right, my dude!"

"Peanuts did Daddy tell you he was gonna be a star?"

"What you mean by that?"

"He's going to sing. He got a record deal."

"A record deal!" Peanuts screamed. "No! He didn't tell me that. Yo Daddy, what's up man? You got a deal?"

"Well it ain't official yet, not until I sign some contracts. But yea. My girl here she pulled some strings and here I go!"

"Wow! I don't have no words to say. That's out of this world kid! Aye yo! We all going out to eat. This is a celebration! The Turfs won their first game and one of their coaches is gonna be a star. Wow!"

Lil Kareem overheard the news and was so excited that he told the others. They were all cheering for Daddy. Jasmine looked around and saw how much everybody was cheering for Daddy, and she loved it. She couldn't help from smiling and feeling warm inside. Was she falling in love with this man?

Someone else was looking at Daddy while he was being cheered. And a look of disdain was on Peanut's face, as well as jealousy.

After the game, Daddy had driven Jasmine home. They sat in front of her building watching the snow fall in large white flakes. It was coming down so heavy and fast that you could hear the silence. It was beautiful.

Jasmine being the first to break the silence said, "I love snow. It's so pretty when it's coming down like this. It's like a picture from a Hallmark Christmas card."

"Yea it is," Daddy replied.

"I see that a lot of people look up to you, especially, umm, what was his name?"

"Kareem?"

"Yes, Kareem. Every time he made a basket, he looked your way to see the expression on your face. And you yourself were thrilled when he made it. I see a strong relationship between you two."

"Yea. I like all the kids in The Boys Club, but there's something special in Kareem. I see a lot of me in him. I give him a little more attention, I guess, because his father is away in jail. So I kinda took to him."

"I see. Well, it's a good thing, you doing what you do with those boys. I like it."

The silence was back, but only for a few minutes.

"Do you like hot cocoa?" Jasmine asked.

"Of course I like hot cocoa in this weather. Heck yea!"

"I could make some. So you want some?"

"Yea, why not?"

They both got out of Daddy's car and went upstairs. Jasmine's apartment was spacious and unique. It was like being in a mini museum with all of the artwork that was displayed all around. Its French style decorations gave the impression that you were in Paris somehow. It was a lovely place to call home, and Jasmine appreciated her sanctuary every moment. This was where she felt most peaceful and at ease, escaping from the demands of the world. But she felt different this evening. Was it because, for the first time, that a man was in the presence of her own home?

"You have a lovely place here, Jasmine," Daddy said, still exploring the apartment. "This place is big. And you said that you live here alone?"

"Well not exactly all by myself. Spirit stays here with me."

"Spirit?"

"I have a cat named Spirit."

"Oh, a cat. Still it's kinda' big for one person, and a cat."

She brought him his cup of hot cocoa and sat down next to him.

"Mmm this hot cocoa is good. What kind is this?"

"French Vanilla from Swiss Miss."

"Man this tastes good."

"I'm glad you like it. So, Superstar, do you have any songs written?"

"Yea. I got a lil somethin' somethin'."

"Are you nervous about your new success?"

"A little."

"I'm sure you will do fine. I know one thing. You are going to be real busy. There will be shows, interviews, club appearances. People are gonna wanna be next to you."

"You think so?"

"Yep! You are going to be a hit."

"And all because of you, Jasmine." He was looking at her. It was dark, but he could see her beauty highlighted by the candles that were lit. Man, she was so beautiful, he thought to himself. He moved a little closer to her.

"I didn't really do anything. Someone would have discovered you anyway, with that voice. But I can say that I'm glad we met."

"I am too," Daddy replied, putting his arm around her.

Even though they were so close that they could hear each other's heartbeat, there was a distance between them. Jasmine was still holding on to her cup of hot chocolate like she was holding onto her past. The grip of her burden was so tight around her that the tension was felt as Daddy tried to hold her. Could she confide in this man? And if she did, what would he think of her and would her past still haunt her? There were so many questions.

"What's wrong?" he asked her.

"Nothing. I'm alright," she lied.

As if Daddy knew that her still holding the cup would tie her hands up, he took the cup from her hands and placed it on the table.

"You feel so tense. Loosen up a bit. I'm not gonna bite you."

She broke away from his hold and went to the window.

"Look. It's still snowing. Your car is covered."

He walked up behind her and put his arm around her waist and whispered in her ear and said, "So I guess I'm trapped here."

The sensation of him being so close and whispering in her ear sent chills through her body. And the thought of him spending the night made her even more nervous. What would the morning be like with him? Did he like cheese in his eggs? Did he like bacon? Hell did he even eat breakfast? More questions.

Those thoughts were interrupted by some sweet soft sounds that were being played in her head. And then she realized that those sounds were her own voice moaning with pleasure as Daddy was laying a thousand kisses on her neck. She was lost. So weak in the knees, she could have buckled if Daddy didn't have her by the waist.

"I can't."

She broke away from him again and sat down on the couch. Puzzled, Daddy stood by the window looking at a distressed Jasmine with her head in her hands, crying and shaking.

❀   ❀   ❀

PEANUTS WAS a brilliant hustler. He had a mind for good business and he knew when to make good deals at the right time. He was what they call street rich. He had spent three years at the New York State Correctional Institution Sing-Sing for stealing cars. During his incarceration, he met his future in the name of Louis Sanchez.

Antonio Rodriguez was a weak nobody piece of shit Dominican who everybody picked on. He looked like poverty itself. A nerd. He had no money order coming in. Not even regular mail. Apparently, no one cared for him. So he lived off of his state pay, eating only what the state provided for the inmates.

One day while Peanuts was using the bathroom he heard noise coming from the other side like somebody was getting beat up. It was none of his business, but he went to check it out. When he got over there, he saw two black dudes trying to take Antonio Rodriguez's manhood.

"Aye yo. What the fuck!" Peanuts grabbed them both up off of him and beat them up with no problem. He was born and raised in Brooklyn, so he knew how to fight. And plus his reputation was known.

"It was none of your business, Peanuts," one of the perpetrators said.

"Well, I made it my business. That shit ain't going down. Not while I'm here. Now get the fuck out."

"Thank you, Padre. I don't know what I would have done without you helping me."

"It's kool, man. I don't play that gay shit. But damn, man. Ain't you tired of people fucking with you? Man, you gonna have to do something. I can't be around all the time."

"It's okay Padre. I'll be fine. Everything will work out just fine. I'll be leaving here soon, Padre. Perhaps I can be of some assistance to you, you know for helping me out."

"It's kool, man. I mean, nobody deserves what was about to happen to you. Don't worry about it. It's nothing."

"But those Padres you beat up. What about them? They will come after you, no?"

"Mister, I go by the name of Peanuts. They know me in here, as well as on the outside. Trust me. They don't want no problems."

"Very well then, Mister Peanuts. My name is Rodriquez. Antonio Rodriquez. I'll be in touch." And in saying that, he walked away.

Peanuts time was up and he was ready for it. He didn't know what he was going to do once he hit the streets. He would be still on parole, so he had to rethink his criminal ways and come up with some other way on getting money. They will be watching as far as stealing cars. The little Dominican dude, he forgot his name, the one he had saved from getting raped offered to help get him a job in a printing shop the last time he had seen him before he got released, but he wasn't interested in working. Besides, the dude was weird. He couldn't even take up for himself.

When he stepped outside the gate, he was a free man, and damn! It felt good. He stretched his hands high in the air and breathed. When he finished he laid his eyes on a black shiny 600 Benz and the owner was calling his name.

"Excuse me, Sir. Are you Anthony Jones?" Peanuts looked at the dude curiously, not sure what to say. This man knew his government name. Who in the hell was he.

"Yea man, but who the fuck... What the hell you want?"

"I work for a man that owes you a favor and he would like to pay you by giving you a ride."

Peanuts would have declined but the Spanish looking cutie that rolled down the rear window made him accept the offer. And to his surprise when he got in the back seat there was another pretty Spanish girl sitting in there.

"Do you want me or her to suck your dick? Or both of us?"

"I..." and before he could answer, both girls was taking his shit out and sucking on it. He came quick.

"Oh no, Papi. You came too quick. We would have to do this again, yes?"

Gasping for air like he was outta breath, he said, "Yes. Yes. Yes."

Peanuts didn't know what in the world had just happened, but he didn't care. All he felt was relaxed and released. The ride in the 600 Benz from Sing-Sing to Manhattan was a luxury, as well as quick. And with the two Spanish Mammies and some brown brandy, he felt like a king.

He got out of the Benz and was greeted by a little Dominican man that he was almost sure that he had seen before, but didn't quite recognize him.

"Well, hello Padre! Nice to see you again."

"Antonio?"

"No. Antonio Rodriguez was someone who I made up. My real name is Louis Sanchez."

"But you look different. You was weak-looking and..."

"I believe the word is deception, Padre. You see, the judicial system was outraged that they couldn't prosecute me on charges that would have sent me away for a very long time. So they had to settle for tax evasion, which is an insult to their intelligence. They have been trying very hard to bring me up on drug charges, of which they have been most unsuccessful. So I am aware that they are good at planting people in prison to get close to you, to be their eyes and ears. This is why I chose to appear weak, to be a nobody. Not like your Gottis who showboat their lifestyles, thus giving themselves away. You don't have to live like a king in jail, Padre. I was content with being Antonio. It was interesting being weak. I am what they call a good actor. Wouldn't you say, Padre?"

"Yea, you sure are. You had me fooled. But those dudes that were beating on you in the bathroom, they was gonna..."

"Rape me, Padre? No, I doubt that. Not when they are paid very handsomely to perform."

"You mean they was acting? But you was bruised and..."

"Deception is a remarkable tool, isn't it?"

"But why me? What part do I play in this?"

"You just happened to come along and help out someone who was a victim of harassment. You had no idea that a game was being played. So when you jumped on them that made the charade all the better. So, I had you checked out and the report that was brought back to me was intriguing. Even though stealing cars is hardly a career someone can rely on."

"Wow! You know about that huh?"

"I have knowledge of things that would surprise you."

"So what now?" Peanuts asked.

"I have an offer that would benefit your future. I understand you know a great deal about Brooklyn."

"Yea, I do."

"Do you know anything about dope?"

"I know a little. I've seen people use it."

"Well, I'm gonna teach you everything you need to know and then you will own Brooklyn."

"You trust me like that?"

"What I trust is the knowledge that I have on you. Need I say more?"

"No. Your words are understood."

It didn't take long for Peanuts to learn about the drug game. He had made more money than he would ever make stealing cars. His relationship with Louis Sanchez grew, as he made them both money. Everything was going well for him. He was the man. He had his main girl, Shay-Shay, and he could have any other chick for that matter. So why did he want Jasmine?

❀ ❀ ❀

SHE WAS a little girl again. The shaking and crying had transported her back into time. The vivid images that came rushing across her mind were so picture clear she thought that it was happening all over again. As well as seeing, she could feel, hear and smell that moment she wished never took place. But it did.

Fourteen years old. Innocent and vulnerable. She was already in distress from her parents having died and leaving her. And now she was trapped under a roof of turmoil. Uncle Raymond, her father's brother, was a drunk, and he had a wife that treated Jasmine like a ragdoll. Having her mother's Indian beauty was like a curse because it gave her uncle's wife a reason to be jealous and beat on her. Her aunt didn't like the way Uncle Raymond looked at Jasmine and at times, he would scorn her for not being pretty like his niece. One night she had decided to tell her uncle how his wife was treating her. He was sitting in the living room pissy drunk, but came alert when he heard Jasmine's voice calling his name.

"Uncle Raymond. Uncle Raymond!"

"Yes, Lil Pooh. What is it?" his rough voice asked.

She could smell the liquor all over his breath.

"Aunt Susan is mean to me," she said.

"Oh she is just mad because she is so ugly and you're a pretty lil thang. That's all sweetheart. Now come here and tell Uncle Raymond what's happened."

She came to him and started to tell him, but he was holding her wrong. He was touching her too soft, not the way an uncle is supposed to touch his niece.

"Come here, sweetie. I won't hurt you," he assured her.

Jasmine was lost and confused. Her private parts were no longer private as her uncle violated her body. He threw Jasmine down on the couch. She was trying to get up, but his force was too great. He started taking down his pants. She wanted to scream, but would it help? No.

He was talking to her saying, "Now you just take this like a good little bitch, and I promise I'll make you a woman tonight. My woman. Your gonna be better than all of your friends to know about the birds and the bees, cause Uncle Raymond is gonna teach ya. I couldn't have your Indian bitch mother, so you will just have to do. Now take it and don't scream and I won't take my belt off and skin you alive."

He smelled so bad she could have thrown up right there. He was inside her and she was so hurt, but not so much from his penetration as from why he was doing what he was doing to her. A family member. She saw her aunt walk by, and she looked so mad that she could see steam coming from her. Jasmine wondered what she would think of her now. Would she care that her own uncle, her husband, would do such a thing? Of course, she would understand.

He was finished with her now. He got up off of her and Jasmine's body was filled with his mess all over her. She felt so disrespected, so lost. He made her promise not to tell anyone. He didn't have to make her. She didn't wanna tell nobody anyway. How could she? She got up and ran to her room. And if what just happened wasn't enough, her aunt was in her room with a small bag packed.

"You need to leave, you little whore. Stealing my man. I knew what you was up to the moment you moved in here. You are nothing but a little slut."

"But Aunt Susan, where would I go? It wasn't my fault!"

And before she could get another word out, her aunt slapped her across the face. Jasmine broke out crying, feeling so broken.

"I don't care where you go, just get the hell outta our lives, so we can be happy again."

Jasmine got her bag and left.

❀   ❀   ❀

"JASMINE? JASMINE? Are you okay?"

She awoke from her little trance.

"You was lost for a second. Is everything alright? Was it me? Did I do something?

"No Michael. It's not you. I'm so sorry about this. It's just that…"

"What? What's wrong? You can tell me. I'm here for you."

His words sounded sincere and reassuring, she thought.

"I was raped when I was 14 years old. My uncle. He raped me."

Daddy's face changed. He said, "Jasmine, I'm so sorry. I…" There were no words that he could say. What was there to say when something like that has happened to a little girl? He understood now why she broke out crying and shaking.

"I know it must be hard hearing that. Just imagine how I feel!"

"It is a shock to me. I'm more mad than anything."

"I didn't know how to tell you. I didn't know whether I would chase you away or..."

"Chase me away? Please! I'm not going nowhere." He hugged her to assure her of that.

"I never had sex apart from what happened to me. I've had boyfriends, but when it came down to being intimate, I wasn't ready or I was scared and they just left me."

"Jasmine, I'm sorry. Had I known, I wouldn't have tried to..."

She cut him off. "There's no way you could have known. It's not your fault. It's just that I like you a lot and when you were kissing me, it felt good. So good. But memories came crashing back."

"Where was your parents when that happened to you?"

"My parents both died in a car accident on my graduation day. I was thirteen years old. So I went to live with my Uncle and Aunt. They took me in. They had no children of their own, so I was lonely as far as no other children around. The night that happened, my aunt threw me out. So I came here to New York to live with my grandparents. To this day, she doesn't know what happened though. No one does. Except you now. The only thing my grandma knows is that I ran away from them and that she was glad to have me."

"Wow!" Daddy said. "You had some life back then."

"Tell me about it! You wanna know something? I feel good, relieved that I shared this with you. It feels like a heavy weight is off my shoulders."

"Good! You can always share with me anything that's bothering you. I'm here for you."

She smiled at the words that Daddy was a saying. She thought that she was in love with him, but there would have to be a time when she was gonna have to have sex with him. Surely he would want that. Hell, she wanted it too! But being traumatized so long by what happened to her, she didn't know how she was going to break out of her cocoon.

Maybe by having sex for the first time the fear that kept her trapped would disappear. Maybe Daddy's kisses and passionate embrace would deliver a freedom she longed for. Maybe he would be her Prince Charming. Just maybe.

It was the middle of the night and Jasmine was awakened by Spirit (her cat) when she rubbed up against her leg. She and Daddy had fallen asleep right there on the couch. Daddy was snoring, not a loud snore, more like a soft one.

How cute, Jasmine thought to herself. He had been wonderful listening to her as she told him about her past. He didn't look at her any different. He just didn't try anything with her after she had revealed what happened to her. He just took her in his arms and they fell asleep.

She thanked him by kissing him on the lips. His lips were smooth. Not chapped. As if that was a good enough reason to kiss them again, she did. She noticed his mouth open up and his tongue came out. Either he was playing sleep, or he was kissing her in his sleep 'cause his eyes were still closed.

He called out her name. "Jasmine, I'm…"

"It's okay. I wanna do this." And she started kissing him again. Daddy put his arms around her. They were both fully awake now, kissing each other. Them kissing each other like that almost took Jasmine's breath away. The kiss was passionate and slow. She could feel her nipples getting hard as well as the juices flowing in the lower part of her body. She felt like she was drowning in a pool 'cause it was that much of a breathtaking moment.

He was kissing her slowly on her neck. Soft moans escaped Jasmine's mouth as Daddy's fingers were exploring her body. They explored each other's bodies like it was forbidden. With soft nervous touches, they were both lost.

Daddy had sex before of course, but not like this. He was taking his time. And every minute was stimulating.

Jasmine, once afraid that the raw memory would ruin her first attempt at making love, did not let it happen. She allowed the electricity between them awaken the feline that was hidden within her. Daddy was kissing her all over. He had started from her perky breasts, which were upright, not saggy at all and beautiful. He kissed her around her navel. But when he got to her love hole, she was no more good. Daddy's kisses around her poo-poo sent chills all over her body. His tongue caressed the inner parts of her body with skill and desire, like he had been wanting to do this for a long time. Jasmine went crazy.

Her climaxing came like rivers of joy. Her first ever. Now it was time to enter her. And when he did, heaven came to earth. Tears came from Jasmine's eyes, but they were tears of happiness. She had done it. She finally exhaled like the movie Whitney Houston played in. Daddy was inside her and he himself was lost in the moment. They shared their love with each other like it was the very thing they were born to do. When Daddy came, he screamed calling her name like he needed her. She felt his cum shoot all up in her and she welcomed it by squeezing his manhood with her muscles, not wanting to let go.

Once again, she came screaming, "Oh my God, Michael, I'm cummin. I'm cummin. Oh God, Michael!"

She held onto Daddy's back with her nails deep inside his skin like she was hanging off a cliff and if she let go she would fall.

Exhausted from a lovemaking that had a new definition, they laid next to each other with a new look on life.

"That was so wonderful," she said. "I never knew that I would feel so free. Michael, you're my hero."

"I wouldn't say all that."

"I'm serious. You are always taking me somewhere; first with your singing, now this."

She hugged him and just smiled. She was happy.

Daddy left Jasmine's apartment that morning and felt as if he had just struck gold. He got into his car and headed for his place. Yep! It was certainly a beautiful day, he thought to himself. He drove up to his place and a shiny black S550 Benz was parked right outside in front of his house. A female emerged out of the passenger side.

"Damn! It's about time you showed up. I need my shit."

Oh fuck. It's Cindy. Daddy said to himself and she had a mink on. Nice.

"Wow. Whatever happened to 'Good Morning' or maybe 'How have you been?'" he shot back at her.

"Nigga, please. You know damn well I ain't never been that type of bitch. So open the door so I can get my shit and go."

They went inside and she gathered up all of her things and started to leave out the door.

He asked her, "So where's my key?"

"What key'"" she shouted.

"My house key. You know... the one to open the front door?"

"I been left that fucking key. I don't have no key."

"Cindy, you never left shit. So where is my key?"

"I done told you nigga. I don't have no fucking key. Now let go of my arm."

Stacks saw the confrontation, got out of the Benz and came to the door. "What's the matter, baby?"

"He won't let go of my arm."

"A yo motherfucker. Let go of her arm."

"All I want is my key."

"I told you, I don't have no fucking key."

"Listen, dude. Get the fuck off of her."

When stacks grabbed Daddy, Daddy pushed Stacks almost off the steps. Stacks came rushing toward him, but Daddy was ready for him. Stacks tried to throw some punches at him, but Daddy blocked all of them coming back with his own. He connected.

Daddy had never been no punk, so he could fight his ass off. His punches were hard against Stacks' face. He broke his nose. Blood was gushing from his nose like a broken water fountain.

Stacks covered his nose with his shirt, yelling out and saying, "Oh shit! My nose! My fucking nose!"

Stacks ran to the car and tried to get his nine out the glove compartment. But Cindy was saying to him, "Baby, no. Not here. Not now. It's too many people out here."

With all of the commotion and noise, people had come out of their houses and were looking out their windows.

"That's my word, you bitch ass motherfucker. You dead! I'mma kill your bitch ass. My word is bond. You dead!"

Now Stacks was no fighter, but he was notoriously known for using his gun and when he said he was gonna kill you, he wasn't bluffing. Daddy's neighbors were afraid for him. They knew of Stacks' reputation and they didn't wanna' see nothing happen to their friend. Daddy was well liked in his neighborhood.

The broken-nosed Stacks and his old flame drove off. Blood was everywhere. Daddy stood on his doorstep and watched them. He had to watch his back.

✿ ✿ ✿

"DADDY BROKE Stacks' nose this morning," she told Shay-Shay.

"For real? Damn for what? What happened?"

"Over me," she lied. "Daddy don't want to let go of this pussy, but it's over. I told him and he couldn't take it."

"So he punched Stacks in the nose for that?"

"He tried to grab me. Stacks didn't like that, so he shoved Daddy off me and they started fighting."

"I know you was loving every minute of that. Two niggas fighting over you. So Daddy want you back?"

"Yep. That nigga know this pussy good."

"You know Stacks is gonna kill Daddy," Shay-Shay said.

"I got Stacks. He listens to me. I'm not gonna let that happen."

"Yea, cause you don't wanna see your soon-to-be husband go to jail for killing your ex, who's gonna be a superstar."

"Fuck you talkin' 'bout?"

"Daddy. He's got a record deal. Why you didn't tell me that nigga could sing?"

"A record deal?" Cindy said surprised.

"Yep."

"When the fuck this happen?"

"I don't know. Sometime last week. Some girl hooked him up."

Cindy remembered when she found a card with some bitch's name, Jasmine Green, saying that she could help get him a deal or something like that. But she didn't think it would go down.

"Damn! Word, Shay-Shay."

"Yep. That nigga got a deal. Ain't that something?"

"Yea that is something," Cindy said, but in a low voice.

Her mind was racing in all directions. She was hit hard with this news. That nigga was getting ready to hit it big and she had left him. Well, she wasn't about to let him go to the top without her being there with him. He owed her, she thought to herself. She would go to him. Seduce him like she knew she could and he would accept her back. She had that kind of magic. Luckily she had held on to his key. She had kept it, just in case her and Stacks didn't work out. Yep. She had a plan and her plan would work, no matter what.

Damn. I'm a sly, foxy bitch, she said to herself. She was determined to have it all, whatever it took.

❀   ❀   ❀

PEANUTS DROVE up to a house that was looking like it came straight out of the Rich and Famous Magazine. It was big and beautiful. He had never been in the Hamptons, and now he was inside one of the richest neighborhoods, and all of the houses he had passed to get to this one were just as big. He wanted to live out here. Louis Sanchez had invited him to dinner.

He had been working for Sanchez for a while now, so things must be going real good for his boss to invite him to his palace.

"Padre! Welcome, welcome! Did you have a hard time finding the place?"

"Na, na. It was easy. The directions was on point."

"So have you ever been out in the Hamptons before?"

"Na, but this place is nice. I could live out here."

"And one day, you will, Padre. One day, you will."

"Oh, here you go." He handed Sanchez a briefcase with $500,000 inside of it. Sanchez passed it to one of his guards.

"You're not gonna count it?"

"It's all there, Padre. No need to count it. So tell me, Padre: How are you these days? I see that business has been good for you. You have come quite a ways from a car thief to a successful businessman."

"Yea, business is good. Business is real good. Our product is the best on the streets. There's no competition."

"We aim to please, Padre Peanuts. We aim to please. And since you have been doing such a great job, I have a gift for you. Come, let's take a walk out back."

They walked in the back outside and what Peanuts laid his eyes on almost took his breath away.

"What's the matter, Padre? You look like you saw a ghost."

"Is that the gift?"

"It is yours, Padre."

❀   ❀   ❀

SUCCESS WAS on its way and in a hurry. He couldn't stop if he wanted to. Daddy was at Def Jam recording his first single (Love Caught Me Slipping). It would become number one in just a couple of weeks, once it hit the radio. He was definitely on his way. He had signed a three-year contract with Def Jam and they had already given him his first check. They knew what they had, so they invested in his future. When Daddy had the check in his hand, he could not believe his eyes. He had not ever seen that much money at one time. The check was for $100,000. Of course, it would be deducted from his royalties, but with the money that he would be getting, it wouldn't hurt him at all. He called Jasmine to tell her the news.

"Hey Sweetheart, how is my princess doing this morning?"

"Hey back to you, my Prince Charming. What's up?"

"I recorded my first single today and they gave me a check already. Would you believe that?"

"Get out! Really baby? That's good!"

Jasmine was surprised at herself, calling Daddy baby. Was she in a relationship? She thought.

"Yea, Sweetheart. I wanna celebrate. I'm going to see my mother. No wait. Let me come pick you up first and then we'll go over to my mother's. That way, you can meet her and then we will go out and celebrate. Okay?"

"Sounds kool to me. I'll be ready at 1:00 today."

"Good. See you then."

They were in front of his mother's house getting ready to go in, when Jasmine stopped and turned Daddy's face to hers and kissed him on the lips and whispered, "I love you, Michael."

"I love you, too, Jazz." She liked the way he shortened her name, so she smiled.

"I'm so nervous going to meet your mother, I'm shaking."

"You have nothing to worry about. My mother is going to love you. Watch."

They entered the house and were greeted by Mrs. Flowers.

"Michael! Son, why didn't you tell me you were coming by? I could have prepared something to eat. And you brought me a rose."

They were puzzled when she said that, 'cause Daddy didn't have no rose in his hand.

"Huh?" he said.

She let go of her son and hugged Jasmine. "I'm talking about this beautiful young lady here. She looks just like a flower from a garden nowhere on this earth."

Jasmine quickly blushed.

"Look at her. She is so beautiful, Michael. What's your name, Sweetheart?"

"Jasmine."

"And a pretty name to match the face. How sweet. So that means my grandbaby is gonna be extra beautiful."

"MA!!" Daddy screamed.

Jasmine's mouth was wide open and she couldn't help from smiling and chuckling at what Mama Flowers had just said.

"Oh, boy. Be quiet. I'm just kidding."

"No you not, Ma. You always gettin' on me about grandchildren."

"Okay, okay. You got me there. What you trying to wait till I'm dead and gone?"

"We'll get you a couple, Mrs. Flowers," Jasmine said and winked at Daddy.

Daddy looked at her shocked and said, "What is this? Y'all double teaming me?"

He was smiling. Jasmine was even surprised herself at saying that. Guess she felt comfortable with Mama Flowers' lovable spirit.

"Michael, I like her already. Call me Mama from now on, Jasmine."

"Ma, I got some good news for you."

"Good news? What good news?"

"I got me a record deal, Ma. And I just recorded my first single today and here's the proof."

He showed her the check and Mama Flowers eyes went crazy.

"You are kidding, right? Is this some kind of joke?"

"Nope," Jasmine said. "Our boy here is a Rock Star."

"Oh my Lord! God done smiled on you, son!" She started crying with joy. "Oh, how I wish your father could be here for this. He would have been so proud of you. I can't wait to tell the people at the church."

"Oh boy!" Daddy said. "Anyway, as soon as I deposit this in the bank, I'm gonna give you some money, okay, Mamma? Me and Jasmine gotta run. We are going to celebrate."

Jasmine nudged his arm and told him to ask his mother did she wanna come

"Oh, Ma? Do you wanna go with us?"

"No thank you son. I got lots a work to do. You two lovebirds go on ahead."

"Okay, Mama." He kissed her on the cheek and headed for the door.

"Excuse me, young lady?"

Jasmine smiled and said, "Sorry," and kissed Mama Flowers on the cheek, as well.

"Your mother is so nice. She has a free spirit. She's so warm and happy."

"Yea, she's cool."

"How 'bout your father. Is he as nice as her?"

"He was."

"Was?"

"He's dead."

"I'm so sorry. I ..."

"It's okay, you didn't know."

"How long has he been...?"

"He's been dead now over 15 years. He died a hero back when he was in the Army. He saved two little kids. He tried to go back and save more that was trapped in the fire, but never made it back out."

"Michael I'm so sorry."

"It's kool. I'm way over it now. I could talk about it."

"You must have been proud of him."

"I was. I was. He was my hero, too."

"So where do you wanna go celebrate at?"

"Let's go to the Lyric Love Café."

They was at the café chilling out, laughing, and sipping on a couple of drinks when Jasmine recognized someone.

"Tricia! What in the... Girl, what you doing here?"

"Hey Girl," Tricia yelled back at her, hugging her friend.

Daddy could not believe his eyes. He was in a mess.

"This is my friend that I have been telling you about."

"Daddy!!"

"You two know each other?"

"What's up, Tricia?" He said that like it hurt him.

"Yea, we know each other from the hood. What's up Daddy Mike?"

There she go, calling me that, he said to himself.

"Nothin', just chillin'," he said with a false smile.

"So this is a nice celebration. We all know each other and you surprising me by coming to a poetry spot, Tricia."

"Yea, a friend of mine is performing here, so he asked me to come and what do you mean by celebration?"

"This is my friend who has the record deal."

"Oh shit, for real?"

"Yep, for real!"

"I didn't know you could sing, Daddy."

"I do a little."

"Get the hell outta here."

"Oooh this drink got me gotta use the bathroom bad. I'll be right back."

"You want me to come?" Tricia asked.

"No, I'm good. Stay here. Talk to Michael so y'all can say good things about me."

Jasmine got up and went to the bathroom.

"Look, Tricia. I know you don't like me, but can you please don't say nothing about Cindy to Jasmine?"

"Oh, please, Daddy. I didn't say I didn't like you. Where did you get that impression?"

"Huh? I thought... Never mind, just don't say..."

"I'm not gonna say nothing. Jasmine my girl. Me and Cindy we kool, but Jazzy is my best friend and I don't wanna hurt her. She's happy with you. She brags about you all the time. Naw, I'm not gonna say shit. Just don't hurt my girl.

"I have no intentions."

"Besides, Cindy is full of shit anyway. You better off with Jazzy."

Jasmine came back from the bathroom. "So did y'all talk good about me?"

They both stared up at her and smiled, "Of course we did, sweetheart. Of course we did!"

Daddy drove Jasmine home after they left the café. He wanted to take her to his place, but thought it best not to do that because he didn't know what Stacks was up to and he didn't want Jasmine in between his mess. Besides he had to rise early to go down to the studio and if he had brought her home, he probably wouldn't have gotten no sleep. But he was horny as hell. He had been drinking. Mixed with all the excitement, plus some brown liquor. Yea, he could have used a little pleasure, but still he knew Stacks was a killer and he wanted to keep Jasmine safe.

When he walked into his house, he stopped and was startled at what he saw.

"What the fuck!"

Cindy was laying on the couch with her legs wide open, while a pretty Latina chick was eating her pussy. She saw when Daddy entered. She smiled and licked her lips. She told him to come here with her finger. Daddy stood there frozen in time, not knowing what to do. While all along JoJo (his friend between his legs) was throbbing to get out. He did not want to give in. And he wouldn't. He couldn't.

Cindy, knowing that she would lose the battle by herself had brought along a weapon. After what had happened with Daddy and Stacks, and that she had left him. She knew that he would not wanna be bothered with her. She also knew his fantasy.

"You not gonna come join us?" Cindy said that between moans.

She whispered in the other chick's ear. "Go bring that dick over here."

The other chick got up and sashayed over to Daddy. She pulled him towards the couch where Cindy still laid. JoJo was brick hard by now and he was ready to enter any hole that was pointed in his direction. The other chick unzipped his zipper, his dick jumped out like it had been caged for too long.

"I can't do this," Daddy said.

"But you want to and you will," Cindy shot back.

He started to say something else, but moans came out of his mouth first. The other chick was sucking on JoJo deliciously while Cindy just watched for the moment. Daddy had his eyes closed and was fully into it now. He had no choice 'cause the other chick was giving him a blow job that was out of this world. He felt his shirt being ripped apart by other hands. It was Cindy. It was time for her to join in on the fun.

Daddy was no more good. He had her tongue caressing his body and it felt good. His nipples and dick were being licked, sucked and kissed, all at the same time.

"Damn, fuck, shit!!" He cursed Cindy for being so goddam good for what she does.

This bitch was skilled in sexual seduction. And once again, she had him at the balls. (Literally). Just when he thought he was about to come, the other chick stopped and started kissing on Cindy's neck. They both left Daddy alone and were engaged in a kissing match, their tongues fighting for position. Daddy stood there massaging himself loving every minute of this escapade.

Daddy joined in and they were all intertwined with one another. There was so much touching, licking and sucking going on that their bodies were inflamed with lust. He was in pleasure land. Right inside his house. Suddenly, he heard a set of noises cry out of both women. They were coming. And coming strong. Daddy kept pleasing the two women as they screamed out their orgasms. It was like a symphony.

The two women left their positions to attack Daddy and they did with a lustful revenge. They kissed him all over his body. It was intoxicating. Cindy was giving him a blow job, while the other chick kissed his nipples. He couldn't take it any longer. He came. His yelling could have woken the whole neighborhood. Cindy continued to take all his juices until there was no more to take.

Daddy collapsed on the couch 'cause his knees had given in. He was done. It was done. Cindy had devised a plan and it had worked. Sex was always a weapon that could be used to get one's way. And Cindy knew how to use that weapon like a pro. She could be his manager. No, she could be his producer. No, handle all of his affairs. She was thinking all of this, as money signs paraded her mind.

"Did you like what just happened?" Cindy whispered in his ear.

"I'll let you know when I come off my high."

Cindy smiled. "You took care of two women. You're a beast."

She was massaging his ego now. Damn this chick was good. "Me and JoJo, we make a good team."

He might as well have stood up and beat on his chest the way he was gloating.

"Y'all sure do. JoJo was hard as steel when you walked in. I saw him."

"Yea, I was shocked to see what I saw."

"So, I heard that you are a superstar."

"Oh, yeah? Where you hear that from?"

"It's all over. Everybody know."

"So now I know what this is all about."

"What happened tonight was gonna happen anyway. It don't have nothin' to do with nothin'. I knew that you wanted a threesome and I wanted to give you one. That's all."

"C'mon, Cindy. We both know why you're here. You heard that I got a record deal and now you wanna try to ease back into my life. You left for that nigga Stacks for what he can do for you. Now you know that I hit it big, you wanna give me some love."

"Boy, please. Ain't nobody thinking about your career. I just wanted some of that…"

"Cindy, be real for a change. That's all I'm asking."

"Okay, Daddy. Okay. Yes, I heard about your little deal, and technically I never left you. Some of my stuff is still here."

"But you came and got everything…"

"No, I didn't. You're still here."

"Come on, Cindy. We can't do this. I have someone in my life now. I mean it was good while it lasted, but I'm good now. And I knew you still had my key, so why you let that bullshit go down with me and Stacks?"

"You don't have to worry about Stacks. I got him. So who's the bitch you think I'm gonna stand by and let take my place?"

"Her name is Jasmine and we doing Alright. So I don't need no bullshit with you. She likes me and I like her. So that's that."

"So you jut gonna fuck me and think that it's over just like that? Naw, fuck that. It don't work like that."

"Fuck you. You came here in my house. Remember? I didn't come begging."

"Yea, well you could have stopped me and told me that you didn't want none. Shit you used me."

"Cindy, please. Ain't nobody used you. You welcomed yourself into my house, you and your friend."

"So you just gonna do this to me, just throw me out of your life like that?"

"I mean, we still kool. But just not like before. You got your boyfriend Stacks and I got me somebody. No hard feelings."

"But I want you."

"Why? Because you know about the record deal?"

"No 'cause I miss you."

"Why didn't you miss me last week when you came here to get your shit?"

"I don't know. I just…"

"Yea, I know, Cindy. It's over and that's that."

"Daddy, I'm not giving you up. And besides you owe me."

"Owe you what? I don't owe you shit!"

"All of the shit I did for you, and you forgot."

"Cindy you getting high on something, cause I don't owe you nothing!"

"So it's like that."

"Yea, it's like that."

"You know what Mr. Hot Shit. You still ain't shit, and you gonna give me what's mine believe me, I'll get it."

"Yea, yea. Just go please and leave my key this time."

"Here! Take your fucking key. C'mon, Lisa. Let's get the fuck outta here."

Cindy and her friend left. She was pissed. She thought that she could just fuck her way back into Daddy's life. But he wasn't having it. He really must be in love with Jasmine. Either that or he got smart. Cause he used to let Cindy get away with her seducing him, but not this time. He had won this battle, but knowing Cindy who was vindictive, she is not going to let up. Naw, not while knowing that Daddy was about to be rich. No she won't quit. She will come up with something.

❀   ❀   ❀

PEANUTS COULD not believe that Luis Sanchez had blessed him with a brand new Benz. It was a 2008 custom made S550, the color of butter. The inside was lime green and the softest leather that Peanuts had ever touched. He loved it. The automobile had been imported from Germany and only a select few had them. His Benz could not come close to this one. Of course, it had a built-in navigation system and it was bulletproof. But what Peanuts didn't know, was that a bugging device was planted inside the steering wheel. Luis Sanchez prided himself on knowing the whereabouts of those who worked for him, as well as what they were talking about and to whom.

So the GPS system and bugging device would come in handy. He trusted no one in this cutthroat business, so he had to take precautionary measures. So the gift to Peanuts was very necessary, necessary indeed. Peanuts pulled up to the KitKat Klub and saw Cindy standing outside. Her eyes got big as shit when she saw him get out of his brand new Benz.

"Oh shit! Peanuts, when the fuck you get this and where the fuck you get it? This shit is fire!"

"You like it?"

"Like? I fucking love it. Ain't nobody in New York got this. You got it going on, Peanuts."

"I do what I do, Ma. You know me."

"I know that's right."

"Where's Shay-Shay?"

"Oh she left early. She said she had something to take care of."

"So why the fuck she didn't call me?"

"She tried to, but your phone was off or something. Sure you ain't fucking around on my girl?" She said that while massaging his dick.

"Let's go for a ride," Peanuts said. His dick was hard now.

"Sure, where to?"

"The Hoe tell," Cindy smiled and jumped in the car.

"Damn Peanuts. You was fucking me like you had something to prove."

"You wasn't no slouch neither. Damn you kept my shit hard!"

"Am I better than Shay-Shay?"

"Does pork come from a pig?"

They both laughed.

"I came so many times. I think it was a mixture of riding in that Benz and riding you. That Benz turned me the fuck on."

"Word."

"Fuck yea. I should be the bitch on the passenger side all the time."

"Now how is that gonna be? You and Shay-Shay are girls."

"I know, I know. I'm just saying. It should be me, that's all."

"I ain't gonna front. You are sexy as hell and you're a hustling chick that is down for whatever."

"You think so?"

"I know so. I saw how you used to hold down Daddy."

"Don't mention that bitch ass nigga's name."

"Damn, it's like that?"

"He get on my fuckin nerve. Just because he got a record deal, he swear he hot shit."

"It ain't like that with him. He's kool. That's still my boy."

"If you think so."

"What you mean by that?"

"Daddy never had the hustle in him like you do. He used to tell me that you thought you was the shit with your Benz," she lied.

"He said that?"

"Yup. He didn't wanna hustle with you 'cause you would be his boss and he hated that idea."

"Get the fuck outta here. Word?"

"Word. He said that when you came home and got it on, your head got too big. He used to wish that he had the connect. That you got lucky. He told me when y'all was growing up, he used to take up for you and that you was really a punk."

Peanuts could not believe his ears. Was all this true?

"Does that sound like your boy?"

"I guess that really ain't my boy, like that."

"Peanuts, you're way better than Daddy could ever be. Just because he got a record deal, don't mean shit. He not all that."

"You just saying that cause he don't wanna fuck with you no more."

"No, I'm serious, Peanuts. You always had it going on, and you handsome as hell. Shay-Shay is pretty, but she ain't down for whatever. I am, though. We should be a team."

"I could use someone like you on my team."

"So let's do this then, and watch and see how I will have your back."

"No doubt. No doubt. You know what I wonder?"

"What?"

"I wonder if Daddy would let me be his manager."

"I betcha' he say no, that he already got somebody in mind."

"I'mma call and just ask him, just to see what he say."

Peanuts called Daddy's cell phone. He wondered if he was with that pretty bitch, Jasmine.

"Yo. What up my dude. How's my superstar homeboy?"

"Yo what up Peanuts. What's the deal? I'm at the studio now doing my thang."

"Word. That's kool kid. Aye yo. Listen, right. I was just thinking that maybe I could help you out, like be your manager or something, you know? Get into the music game with you."

"What you know about music, Kid. This ain't the drug game, of which you got that down to a science. Besides I already got a manager. And you won't have to work anyway. Once I really get up there, I got you. We boys."

"Damn my nigga. I thought at least I could have been your manager or something."

"But I already got one kid."

"Yea, Yea."

"Aye yo. Look. I gotta run. They calling me for the video shoot. One, my nigga?"

"Aight kid one."

"See what I told you? He kicking you to the curb. He gonna forget that y'all ever grew up together. Watch. Especially if he thinks you still hustling. He not gonna wanna mix that with his music career."

"You might just be right."

"I know I'm right."

She climbed on top of him and said, "Daddy could be destroyed. We don't need him or Shay-Shay. The world could be ours."

He felt himself getting hard again as Cindy was rubbing up against his manhood.

"What do you mean destroyed?"

"He doesn't mean shit to you or me, Peanuts, baby. And I know we don't mean shit to him. I could come up with some story that the tabloids would love to print that would destroy his career before it ever started."

"You are an evil bitch. I'm glad you're on my side."

"No, I just wanna be on top with you, that's all. Now give me some of this dick while it's nice and hard."

❀   ❀   ❀

SIX MONTHS had gone by and Daddy was a big hit. His record sales were soaring to the top. Talk show hosts even wanted to get in on the action and invited the new up and coming rising star on their shows. His single, "Love Caught Me Slipping" was being played on radio stations all over the country. He was in demand. Jasmin sat at her desk reading an article on him and was overwhelmed with the success that had come so fast. She had known that he would make it, but not at this rate. Everybody loved him. There even was a story on him that was insulting and downright dirty that the tabloids had put out there. But there was always somebody out there to assassinate rising stars' characters when there was so much good stuff about them and their success. There were always lies to be told. She didn't believe any of that mess.

Daddy had wanted her to stop working because he was making enough money now to support them both. But she had declined the offer. She loved working, and besides her company depended on her. She was working so hard and with the excitement of Daddy's singing career, she hadn't even noticed that her period hadn't come in a couple of months.

"Jasmine, you have been looking ill lately. Are you okay?" Miss Johnson asked her.

"Yes, Miss Johnson. I'm fine. It's probably the 24-hour virus. I'll be okay."

"You still work too hard, my dear. You should take some time off and get checked out. You never can tell these days with all this stuff going round."

"Okay, Miss Johnson, I will."

"Don't okay me child. I'm serious." She leaned over to Jasmine and said, "You should go take some time and enjoy life with that superstar boyfriend of yours and have lots of sex. He's so handsome!"

Jasmine was shocked that Ms. Johnson had said the "S" word.

"When you see him, give him a big kiss for me, will you?"

"Yes, Miss Johnson, I will." Jasmine said smiling.

"Okay, I'm leaving now and I don't want to see you in here tomorrow. You get checked out. Love you! Bye."

Miss Johnson was right. Maybe she had better go get herself checked out. She had been throwing up, for no apparent reason and her breasts was getting bigger. Yep she would definitely go to the clinic tomorrow.

"There's nothing to worry yourself about, Ms. Green. You're perfectly all right," the doctor had told her.

"But why have I been throwing..."

"You're pregnant, Ms. Green."

"Pregnant?"

"Yes, pregnant!"

Oh my God! How did this happen? Stupid me, she said to herself. She knew how it happens, but when did it happen? *We only had sex a couple of times. My God, I'm pregnant.* She thought to herself. *Wow!*

"Dr. Haden, thank you."

"No problem, Ms. Green. Glad I could help. But just take it easy and come back on your regular checkups, and you will have a healthy baby, I promise you."

"Okay, Dr. Haden, I will."

She couldn't wait to tell Michael, but he was in Florida recording his next single.

I'm gonna call him, she said to herself and tell him the good news. She wondered how he would take it, *would he be happy? Would he be mad?*

She could contain the excitement no longer. She took her cell phone out and pushed his speed dial number.

"Hello sweetheart."

"Hey my sweet potato pie." She liked when he called her that knowing that was his favorite pie.

"Hey baby, there's something I want to talk to you about. It can't wait and you're all the way in Florida."

"Well, baby. I'm gonna be here all week. Can't it wait until I get home?"

She was disappointed. She wanted to tell him now, but she didn't want to do it over the phone. She wanted to see his face when she told him.

"Well, I guess it could wait. I..."

"Unless you want to come down here with me?"

"Could I? I mean, I don't want to be in the way or anything like that."

"In the way? Please sweetheart. You're my charm if anything. You'll give me inspiration."

She smiled when he said that.

"Okay, I'm going to go pack some things and take the next flight out."

"Okay. Just call me and let me know when your flight touches down so I can have someone pick you up."

"Okay, baby. Bye."

Jasmine was so excited she didn't know what to do. She was going to Florida to be with her sweetheart. She was jumping up and down like a kid; when she remembered what she was going there for, she stopped. She didn't want to hurt the baby. *My baby. Michael's baby. Our baby*, she thought.

Florida was beautiful. There were palm trees all over and Jasmin was taking it all in. She hadn't been to Florida before, so everything was new to her. The driver was there to pick her up like Daddy had told her. She couldn't wait to hug her Michael. She had wanted to be different from everybody else that called him Daddy, so she continued calling him by his name, Michael.

When she saw him, she hugged him like she hadn't seen him in two years. He did the same and gave her a long passionate kiss. They were so much in love with each other. Nothing else could be better than this. Having a beautiful lady on his side and a single that had been a number one hit in the country for two months was incredible. Now he was working on his second song of his first album.

"So what's this you wanna talk to your baby about?"

"I'm pregnant."

"Pregnant? Like a baby pregnant?"

Jasmine shook her head yes and said "Uhmm."

"Oh wow! Oh shoot! A baby! I'm going to be a Daddy, a father! Oh shoot!"

He picked up Jasmine all excited and started swinging her around. He stopped quickly and said, "Oops, can't hurt my family. Come sit down. Are you okay? Are you alright? I'm sorry I ..."

"I'm okay silly."

"Wow a baby" he shouted out. "Hey, everybody. I'm gonna be a Daddy. I mean a father! I mean... oh shoot Jasmine's pregnant!"

Everybody was shouting and clapping for the happy first time gonna be parents. Daddy was gleaming. He kissed Jasmine's stomach and put his ear to it to hear the baby's heartbeat. Then suddenly he grabbed Jasmine by the hand and told his manager, Bobby Wilson to come go with him.

He had his driver drive them all down to the best jewelry store in town called Diamonds are Forever. He jumped out of the car and told his manager and Jasmine to wait in the car.

"What is he up to?" Jasmine said.

"I don't know but he's up to something."

It took Daddy twenty minutes to return from the jewelry store. He opened the door, pulled Jasmine by the hand slowly and gently escorted her out of the car. He took out a small black box and got on his knees. Jasmine was getting a little nervous. He opened the box and Jasmine laid eyes on the biggest diamond she had ever seen up close like this.

"Would you marry me, Miss Jasmine Green?"

Jasmine was all weak in the knees and speechless. She finally got the breath to say, "Yes, Mr. Michael Flowers. I will marry you."

Daddy took the ring out of the box and put it on Jasmine's finger. They hugged and kissed for almost an eternity.

They were married in Florida at a small church, not too far from the studio where Daddy was recording. No matter how hard they tried to keep it a secret, the paparazzi was there to get their pictures. It was big news. An up and coming rising star who was a singing sensation got married and is going to be a father. Yes, it was certainly big news. Daddy would have loved to tell his mother the news himself instead of her hearing about it "through some newspaper", but he understood the business. These people were relentless in getting pictures and news. It was their job. Jasmine, on the other hand, couldn't care less. She was married now. She loved and adored her new husband, not because of his career. She could care less about that. She would have loved him just the same, if he was just a cab driver. She reflected back when they had first met. She had taken to him in a small way. (Something that was in his eyes). Not knowing that it would amount into something as huge as this. *Married. Is this euphoria?* She thought to herself.

They were back in New York now, headed towards Mamma Flowers' house. When they got there Daddy noticed a couple of cars in front of his mother's house.

"Oh boy, here we go."

"What's the matter Booboo?"

"Everything. My whole family is here. We getting ready to be bombarded."

"Oh."

"We should turn around and make a clean getaway."

Jasmine chuckled, "You sound as if we robbed a bank. Is it that bad?"

"You don't know the half."

"Well, well well, if it ain't the Rock Star."

"Hey Uncle Paul, how're you doing?"

"Mike, Mike, why you didn't tell us you got married. We didn't even know that you had a girlfriend. And she's pregnant? Boy you are something else. Keeping good news like that away from the family. I should put you over my knee, you know. You ain't too big to get a beating."

Daddy couldn't even get a word in. That was his aunt Sheila going off with the mouth. She and his Uncle Paul came up from Virginia.

101

"Sheila, give the boy a break and let him at least introduce this fine beautiful pretty lady to us. You can't never keep that mouth shut."

"Oh shut up, Paul. This my nephew. I could talk if I want to. Now, what's your name sweetheart?"

At that instant, Mama Flowers came from the kitchen.

"Daughter-in-law!" Hey sweetheart, hey son. I didn't hear y'all come in. Jasmine is these people bothering you? Come over here child and rest yourself in my chair."

"Everybody, this is my wife, Jasmine. Jasmine, this is my family."

"Hey beautiful, my name is Uncle Paul, and Michael here gets his good looks from me."

"Paul, if you don't go sit your tired old ass down somewhere before your teeth fall out and bite the poor child by mistake with your mouth wide open."

"Now, sweetheart, why you couldn't wait to get married here at your Mama's church? You know I would have loved that."

"It just happened Ma. No big thing. We wanted a small wedding."

"No big thing? See there sis. He done gone crazy, let me put him on my knee, Just then security came in. "Is everything alright, Mrs. Flowers?"" Aunt Sheila protested.

"What you mean, no big thing? My son gets married all the way in Florida and I wasn't invited. Yo Daddy is turning over in his grave."

"Oh come on Ma. Don't be like that. We'll have a big reception at your church, okay?"

"You promise"

"Promise."

Jasmine sat there taking all this in when she was bum-rushed by Mama Flowers and Aunt Sheila, who both wanted to feel her stomach and hear if the baby was breathing.

"I'm gonna be a grandmamma again!" Daddy's big brother and his nephew John John came in from the back yard.

"Well if it ain't Mr. Big Stuff."

"What up Big bro?"

"Hey Uncle Mike Mike? Can I go on tour with you?" Everybody laughed at the toothless John John.

"Sure, you can Sport. You bet you can."

"Hello. I'm his big brother Johnny. It's a pleasure to meet my new sister-in-law."

"Hello my name is Jasmine."

"And I heard we're getting ready to have a lil one."

"Yep and I'm gonna spoil it rotten," Mama Flowers said.

"We know, Ma. Just look at John John. He's no more good." They all laughed.

❄ ❄ ❄

DADDY'S FAMILY wasn't the only ones who heard the news of him getting married and about to become a father. Cindy was reading the article on him and looking at the photos taken of him and his new bride. ON his arm, right by his side clung to him the most beautiful woman she had ever seen. The woman could have easily passed for some princess in a fairy tale story. But that didn't stop her from calling Jasmine every name in the book. She was mad as hell. Jealous was more like it. Here it was that she had his back all this time, and he goes off and marries some other chick, and got her pregnant at that.

103

"How the fuck could he do this to me?" She had thought to herself. Well she would break up their little happiness, if it was the last thing she did. It was time to meet Mrs. Jasmine Flowers. Yes, it was definitely time to meet her. Cindy looked at the photos again and when she noticed Jasmine's ring, she just screamed out loud.

They had been boys forever. And they would be boys forever, according to their pact that they had with one another. They were so close that they used to spend the night at each other's houses, played and messed with girls together. They were in the same school and same class. When one had a fight they both had a fight. They had each other's back. Cindy had planted a seed in Peanuts' head that would cause him to think otherwise. She had a plan to turn them against one another and it was working.

They were at the remodeled Boys Club courtesy of Daddy. He had bought new basketballs and rims, as well as new uniforms for the team. He even had the floor done. They loved him for everything he did. He did not forget about them just because he had made it big. He still took time out to come by whenever he had time to see about the boys at the club.

"Yo what up, dog?"

"Ain't shit Peanuts. What's up wit you kid?"

"Dam my nigga. You forgettin' about your boy, or what?"

"Now what makes you say that?"

"You go off and get married. You don't let me know and, on top of that, you let some lame ass dude to be your best man. Whassup wit dat?"

"He not no lame, he's my manager and he was there at the time. That's all kid. No biggie."

"But damn dog. You didn't think for a second that I might wanna be your best man while you marry that pretty lil thang?"

"C'mon Peanuts. Man, don't go there with me on this. I had enough with my family already."

"You forgetting about your people, kid. That's not kool."

"Anyway, what's going on with you? How's you and Shay-Shay doing?"

"We kool."

"Word."

"Yea so what's up with this music shit? You gonna let me be in a video or something? Come to your party?"

"You can come to all the parties you want, but the videos is off limits."

"Why? Why they off limits?"

"While you're still dealing, I don't wanna be seen with you in a video that's gonna be all over the place. You never know who's watching. You are big in the streets and I'm not trying to mess my shit up because of that."

"Bullshit. You know how many rappers be having hustlers in their videos?"

"I'm not them."

"Aye yo. You flippin' on me kid. Cindy was right. She ..."

"What the fuck she got to do with anything?"

"Like I said, you forgettin' you people."

"Yo, kid. Don't let her get to you man."

"She don't need to get to me. You showin' me that you don't give a fuck about our friendship, dog."

"Stop hustling and you could go anywhere you want with me."

"I'm just saying dog. You changed, my nigga. You changed."

"Aye yo, Peanuts. I could never forget about our friendship. We grew up together. That means something to me. It's just that I got an opportunity to get out of this hood, man. And I'mma go for this.

You can be right there with me kid, all the way. Just stop selling that shit and let's do it the right way. That's all I'm saying."

Peanuts' phone rang. It was Cindy.

"Look, Dog. I gotta run, but I'll give it some thought about what you was saying. But I'm still tight with you about that best man shit."

Peanuts got in his Benz and drove off. His mind was fucking with him now. Everything that Cindy had told him was sounding more real. Daddy thought that he was above him.

Why the fuck should I quit doing my thang just to be in a stupid ass video here and there while he got all the fame and glory. Fuck that shit, he said to himself.

Even if he wanted to quit, Luis Sanchez would not let him. He was too valuable. He was making too much money for Luis Sanchez, and besides, he knew too much. He recalled some kid from Queens who was making some good money for Sanchez and he had wanted out of the business. Said he was through with selling. Well, Sanchez had smiled and politely said, "No problem Padre. You have done well for me. So well, I am going to give you a bonus of half a mill and a vacation in Florida." No one had heard from or seen the kid from Queens ever again. No. He wouldn't cross Sanchez like that. He didn't want no bonus or a vacation in Florida.

He pulled up in front of the Kid Kat Klub and there she was waiting for him. Shay-Shay was in North Carolina visiting her family, so it wasn't nothing to pick Cindy up from where they both worked. Besides, no reason to hide. She hopped in the Benz with no problem, like it was hers. She handed him a paper bag containing $20,000 in it and kissed him on the cheek.

"Damn, you's a bad bitch."

"The best."

There was some silence between them for a second.

"What's wrong, Boo?"

"You were right about what you said about Daddy."

"Why what happened?"

"We had it out, the motherfucker told me to stop hustling or I can't be in his video. You get this dude?"

"Word. He said that? See I told you. Told you he was on some other shit."

"Fuck that shit. I don't need that nigga. Fuck him and his video. If we wasn't like that, I'll have that nigga's head."

Cindy nodded her head in agreement, with a sly little smile on her face.

Jasmine was inside of the office, sitting at her desk, daydreaming. She could not believe that she was now married. When she had told her boss, Ms. Johnson, the news that she got married and she was pregnant, Ms. Johnson was so happy for her you would think that she was the one that was pregnant the way she carried on. She was saying things like "Jasmine, we gonna have a big baby shower. Jasmine, we gonna have a big celebration for you getting married and so on and so on. Jasmine adored her boss. She had been more than just a boss to her. In Jasmine's eyes, she was like a mother to her. She had been there for Jasmine in more ways than one.

As Jasmine sat there rubbing her stomach, she could have sworn she felt a small movement within her. She smiled. Inside her, life was growing. A life that was part of someone who she loved and was her whole world. Daddy had come into her world and rescued her from her past. She no longer was haunted by memories of long ago. She was free, soaring through life, gently like a mid-September breeze. Her daydreaming was interrupted by the intercom.

"Ms. Green?"

"Yes?"

"There's a Miss Jones here for the job interview."

"Okay, Mrs. Watson, send her in."

Jasmine got up from her seat and extended her hand to Miss Jones.

"Good morning, Miss Jones. Please have a seat."

Cindy sat down in the soft leather chair and was astonished of how beautiful Jasmine was in person. She was even more jealous now.

"So you're here for the editorial position, correct?"

"No, actually I'm here to see you, Miss Bitch!"

Jasmine was startled. "I beg your pardon?"

"Don't try to sound all prissy. You heard me. I'm not here for no job. I'm here to see yo ass."

"I think you should leave."

"You think that you could just come from wherever and take my Daddy?"

"Who?"

"Michael, Bitch. He's mine. He's pussy-whipped and I pussy-whipped him. So don't think that it's a happy ending by him marrying yo' pretty ass."

Jasmine could not believe that this low life was sitting here belching out all of this crap

"Listen, Miss. I don't know who you are and what you want, but you have made some mistake coming into my office smelling like that."

"Smelling like what?"

"Smelling like trash 'cause that's exactly what you are, and I'm pretty sure Michael got rid of his trash long before I came! Now, get out!"

Just then security came in. "Is everything alright, Mrs. Flowers?"

"Yes. But you can escort this young lady off the premises."

"You haven't heard the last of me, Miss Bitch. Watch your back and tell Daddy that Pussykat said hello!"

Daddy was furious when Jasmine told him what had happened to her at work. He could not believe that Cindy would stoop that low as to go up to Jasmine's job and harass her like that. Then again, that was Cindy's MO. She was liable for anything. He wouldn't put anything past her. He was glad that he had purchased a home in New Jersey so that he didn't have to go back to his apartment. Someone had been parked out in front of his house waiting for him to come home, his neighbor Miss Luey had told him. He suspected that Stacks was still looking to fulfill his promise of killing him. He had broken his nose and he didn't want to let that go. But that had been months ago when Miss Luey saw the parked car, and that was it. Still he took no chances, so he bought himself a new house in a rich little neighborhood in Cape May, New Jersey. That way, Cindy or whoever, couldn't get at him and his family.

❀ ❀ ❀

"BUSINESS IS good I see, Padre."

"Yea, things is real good, Mr. Sanchez."

"I see your Rock n' Roll superstar friend is making it real big these days." Peanuts was always amazed at how Sanchez knew so much.

"Yea – he doing him."

"So tell me, Padre. How does it feel to be in power?"

"I mean, it feels good. I'm good."

"You don't have any regrets, do you?"

"Regrets? No. Why do you ask?"

"Sometimes, people get too rich for their own good and they want to move on. Do you want to move on Padre?"

"Mr. Sanchez, I'm with you all the way. I'm not going nowhere."

"It's good to hear you say that, Padre."

"Now, how is the stripper turned hustler working out for you?"

"How did you...? Never mind. She's doing swell. I think she's a valuable asset."

"Do you?" He went over and sat next to Peanuts and whispered, "Be careful of a woman Padre. They have more venom than snakes."

Daddy's album was number one in the country. Almost every song on the album was a hit. Anyone who was somebody in the music industry wanted to do a collaboration with him, even his songwriting skills were in demand. He was definitely a superstar. His friendship with Peanuts was no better than the last time they had talked. The more Daddy's career grew and he was coming in contact with some very successful people, the more he was distancing himself away from negative things of his past life. If Peanuts continued to deal in the streets, Daddy would have no part in that. He did not want to lose out on becoming someone who people around the world love and respected.

Just as well with Peanuts. He was not even thinking about Daddy and his music career. As long as he was making money, he was good. He had everything that he wanted. But sometimes when he saw his longtime friend on TV with his new wife, something inside of him didn't feel right. He was still jealous that Daddy could marry such a beautiful girl like Jasmine and put a baby up in her. He had dreams of bedding Jasmine on several occasions. He was obsessed with her. He wanted her. His relationship with Shay-Shay was dull and boring. She didn't even like the gifts that he had bought her. Any girl out there would love expensive furs and diamonds. But not Shay-Shay. She was content. Cindy on the other hand was different. She had taken his gifts without any problem. He was fucking her, so why not bless her with a little bit of this and that. And even though she was a great fuck, she wasn't his main girl. She was still staying with Stacks. But she couldn't be his anyway, and he didn't want her for his woman anyhow. It just wouldn't work out.

He had only seen Jasmine a few times when he and Daddy were still kool. And each time he saw her, she was stunning. He envied Daddy for all he had accomplished. A beautiful wife, a booming career, a nice home in New Jersey. Yup he was jealous. He could have killed for Daddy's place.

Cindy was still on some bullshit. She had tried ways to sabotage Daddy's career, but none would work. Why was it that she and Peanuts were jealous of Daddy so much? Whatever it was, it was on their minds almost every day, especially when they heard his songs on the radio. They met at their usual spot, the Kid Kat Klub. She hopped in the Benz where they had most of their conversations.

"What's up, Peanuts?"

"Hey, Cin. What up?"

"Damn! What's wrong with you?"

"Ain't nothing."

"Like hell it ain't. The look on your face like you lost your best friend."

"I told you, it's nothing."

Daddy's song had just went off and Cindy caught the last of it.

"It's Daddy ain't it." Peanuts didn't say anything. "He's getting to you. You letting that bitch ass nigga get to you."

"This motherfucker man…"

"I know what you mean. I hate him too. He fucked over both of us, but we got each other."

"Yea. We do. Anyway, what's good, you got that straight?"

"Yea. I took care of it."

"What up with that nigga, Stacks?"

"Shit getting on my nerves."

"Man if I had his territory, I'd have all of Brooklyn."

"There might just be a way," Cindy said with a smile.

❀ ❀ ❀

"BABY, HAVE you been thinking about names for our baby?"

"Not really, sweetheart. It hasn't even crossed my mind."

"What do you wish that it would be?"

"I don't know. A girl maybe."

"A girl, huh? Why do you say a girl?"

"Well, I had this dream the other night that the guys at the studio was passing out cigars with 'It's a girl' on them, so I guess that's a sign or something."

"A dream, huh?"

"Yep, a dream."

"Do you want to know what it is? The doctor could let us know."

"C'mon Jazzy. I told you I wanna be there in the delivery room and be surprised. That's the modern way."

"Okay, okay. I'm just excited, that's all. I can't wait."

"Well, you don't have long. Look at you. You're about to bust wide open!"

"I know...O boy, baby. I just felt it kick."

"For real?" He went over to his wife and touched her stomach.

"Feel right here. Can you feel it?"

"Oh sweet. I felt our baby, Baby. It's kicking."

He had a big ass smile on his face. "Dag. This is something else. We're getting ready to be parents."

She kissed him on the cheek and said, "We sure are BooBoo. I love you.

"I love you too, Jazzy."

"So when do you have to leave for the road?"

"Not until next week. I'm going to Florida to shoot a video."

"So I have you to myself for a whole week?"

"Yep. A whole week."

"So, we can play house?"

"If you want to."

"Good, cause I'm feeling a little horny." He started kissing her and the moans came pouring out of her mouth. She was excited to be in his arms, while he kissed her neck. The foreplay he gave her was nothing short of passionate and pleasing.

It was taking too long though. She wanted him inside her. To feel his manhood going in and out of her, like it was their last time on earth and their lives depended on it this moment. He entered her, but being extra careful, he didn't want to hurt her or the baby. When he touched her insides, she exhaled like she had too much wind inside her and it had to escape her body.

"Oooo baby. Ooo baby. That's it, right there. Keep doing that, right there. Oh my God. This feels good."

"You like this, baby? You like this?"

"Oh God, yes. Don't stop. Please don't stop. Don't ever stop ooo ooo..."

She had her nails in his back real hard. It hurt, but felt good at the same time. That made him pump even more.

"I'm coming Daddy, I'm coming." With her calling him that turned him on. She didn't call him that. She must be mad horny, he thought. He kept pushing his manhood.

"Ooo shit, baby. Ooo shit. I'm coming Ooo oooo my god."

She came and came until tears ran from her eyes. Daddy himself had busted with all the excitement that she was giving him. They laid there spent by their lovemaking.

"Daddy?" he said.

"Oops, that slipped. I know I never called you that, but you're my Daddy."

"Naw. That's alright. I was just shocked, that's all."

"That was off the hook sex right there. I guess cause I'm pregnant it made it more exciting. The doctors said it was all right to have sex during pregnancy."

"So you enjoyed that huh?"

"Hell yea. I love you Daddy," she said and kissed him.

"I love you too baby. Hey baby. Tell me how this sounds."

You make me feel a certain
Way
I've been having this feeling
Every day
I can't sleep or eat
You got me where I can't even breathe
Forever, I'm gonna love you
Right
You give me something more
Than life
You're the one for me
You're the reason I breathe.

"Baby, that sounds hot. You just wrote that?"

"Yea, you inspire me, so I wrote it for you.

"Oh, for real? Oh baby, that's sweet."

"I'm going to the studio tomorrow and record it. I'll add some more to it when I get there to make it a full song."

"That's gonna be another hit. Watch."

He smiled at her excitement. He loved his Jasmine and she loved him. They would never be without each other, as long as he lived.

"Y'all got a badass crib here," Tricia said. "My bad, a badass house. Cribs are only in the ghetto."

"It's too big, I think. I don't need no two bathrooms and a half. And we got four bedrooms. That's a lot of cleaning.

"Girl, please. It's not like you gonna be cleaning them, and one of those bedrooms is gonna be for the baby and then one for me!" Tricia said jokingly.

"You know you are welcome any time. Girl, pregnancy is something else. My back be killing me carrying all of this stomach around."

"You do look uncomfortable. I don't see how you manage."

"Girl I don't know either, but somehow I do."

"You don't know what you're having yet?"

"No, I could have but Michael wanted to wait and see at the time of delivery."

"Where is old Daddy Mike anyway?"

"In New York, at the studio, recording."

"I still can't believe, after all this time knowing that boy, that he would become as big as he is."

"Yea, it's something isn't it? I haven't known him as long as you, but it seems like I have known him for life."

"He gets three hit songs out and all of them are up in the charts; his whole album is gonna be the shit."

"I know they're hot..."

Suddenly something was happening to Jasmine.

"What's wrong, Jazz?!"

"I think my water just broke."

"You mean ..."

"Yep, I think it's time Trish."

"Oh shit!" Tricia was running around in a frantic state.

"Tricia, calm down. Just grab the bag, get the car keys and let's go."

"Okay, okay."

"And make sure you got the cell phone and call Michael on our way over... Oh shoot, Tricia. Let's hurry!"

"Okay, okay."

Daddy was at the studio collaborating with Lucius. Ever since he became a hit, everyone wanted to do a song with him. From Maxie, Jeffrey Jay to Selena Jordan, D-Block to everybody that was already in the music industry who had a name for themselves. His voice as well as his songwriting was in demand. There was even talk about a movie that some producers wanted him to be in, but nothing was solid on that. Yep, Daddy was definitely becoming a legend and he was enjoying every moment of it.

"Aye yo, Daddy. The telephone, man. Pick it up on line three."

"Aight," he said.

"Hello yea, what's up... I can't really hear you sweetheart, hold on. Let me go in the other room," he told her.

"Okay, what's up?"

"It's time baby," Jasmine told him.

Daddy's eyes popped out of his head.

"For real? I'm on my way."

Before Jasmine could tell him, she was almost at the hospital, he had hung up the phone.

"Aye yo, I gotta go. My wife is having the baby."

"Aight, Daddy. Aye yo, you want me to drive you man?" his manager said.

"Naw stay here and I'll call you."

Tricia was an expert at driving. She drove the BMW like a pro and got to the hospital at record speed.

"My girlfriend is about to deliver," she told a nurse. The nurse got a gurney and hurriedly rolled Jasmin in one corner of the labor rooms.

Daddy was at the elevator in a panic. The elevator was taking too long. Shit, he said to himself. He ran down the stairs with his backpack on his back. He got outside and almost forgot where his car was. He found it just when a man with a black hoody approached him and asked him what time it was.

Daddy was in such a rush, surprised that the guy didn't know who he was and didn't ask for no autograph. He rolled up his sleeve exposing his Rolex when the man said, "Damn dude that's a nice watch, let me get that."

Daddy found himself facing a nine glock pointing at him.

"Breathe, Mrs. Flowers. Breathe. That's right. You're doing good." The doctor said.

Jasmine was going through it. She was pushing, breathing, pushing, breathing. While Tricia was by her side holding her hand.

"That's right, push Mrs. Flowers, Push."

"Awwwww, Awwww."

"Push, push! It's coming. Keep pushing."

"Aye yo my man, it don't even have to be like this."

"Shut da fuck up and hand everything over. The backpack too. Daddy slowly took the watch off and handed it over to the man and he took the back pack off his shoulder and slowly gave it to him. But before the man could take it from Daddy's hand, he swung the bag and hit the dude in his face. They were tussling over the gun that was still in the guy's hand. Suddenly, the gun went off. Daddy was stooped over holding his stomach while blood was gushing out. The man fled the scene.

Everybody who was up in the studio had heard the shot and came downstairs to see what had happened. They knew that Daddy had just left the building. Daddy's manager was the first to see Daddy laying on the ground bleeding to death.

"Somebody call an ambulance quick. Hurry! He's still alive! Aww shit!"

Everybody was crying. The police had arrived to the scene rather quickly. They gave orders not to crowd the victim so that he could get air. The paramedics had arrived and put a bloody Daddy inside the van and rushed him to the hospital. By the time they reached the hospital, Daddy had died of a gunshot wound to the stomach.

"Mrs. Flowers, congratulations. You have a healthy and beautiful little girl," the doctor was proud to say.

"Aww" said Tricia. "I am a godmother." She started dancing like she had the baby herself.

"Can I see her, doc?"

"Yes. You may. Here you go."

"She's gorgeous."

"Do you know what you're going to name her?"

"No not yet. I am going to wait on Michael. He should be here soon."

Soon would never come. A security guard was watching the news when a special bulletin came across the screen.

"Oh shit. Aye yo that new R&B singer, Daddy, just got killed in New York. Oh wow!" Tricia couldn't believe what she just heard. She started crying. How in the world was she gonna tell her friend?

❀   ❀   ❀

THERE WERE so many people that came out to view the body of Michael Flowers, better known as Daddy that one would think that the president had been assassinated. First there was a public viewing for all of his fans and whoever. Then there was family and a celebrity viewing of the body. Everybody who was somebody within the music world had attended. The world had been crushed by the untimely death of a promising recording artist. His mother had heard the news and instantly had a minor heart attack, which enabled her to see her son off. It was heartbreaking for the family. The funeral was held in the Bedford Stuyvesant section of Brooklyn on Gates Avenue at a large church. It was a private service for family, close friends and the notable. Jasmine was hysterical. She had took the news, as if nothing was wrong. People were concerned about the girl. She had lost her husband and had shed not one tear. They were simply saying that she was in shock, not wanting to believe that he was gone. She would say things like, "Tricia, Michael is gonna put me in one of his videos. Do you wanna be in it?"

Now Tricia knew something was wrong with her friend 'cause she had once told her that she would never be in none of his videos. She felt so sad for her friend.

At the funeral, Peanuts had approached Jasmine and said, "I promise I won't rest until I find out who did this. You have my word."

"Thank you, but let it go Peanuts. The person who did this will get his just do."

Peanuts just looked at her and shook his head yes.

"He was gonna ask you to be godfather to our daughter."

"He was?" Peanuts said surprised.

"Yes, you still could if you want to."

119

"I would be delighted to be the godfather. What's her name?"

"You know, because of all that has been going on, I didn't get a chance to name her yet."

"Well, anyway, if you ever need anything, please let me know. Here's my number."

Jasmine took the number and hugged Peanuts. His hug was reassuring, strong and caring. She felt that Peanuts was there for her, that she could count on him. On the other hand, Tricia had heard of Peanuts and Cindy going out with each other, so she didn't trust him, not one bit.

A week later, someone had tipped the Homicide Department off and led them to Stacks' apartment. They got there with a warrant to search the place and found a semiautomatic glock nine, the same kind of gun that was used to kill Daddy. They arrested Stacks for murder; he was shocked and denied everything. He was tried and because the gun was found out to be the same gun of the murder, he was found guilty and sentenced to 25 to life. Peanuts would take over his territory. Cindy would come up like she never had before...

At their New Jersey home, Jasmine heard the baby crying. She went to get her from her crib.

"Awww. Whassa matter huh, booboo? You want Daddy huh? You miss him, Huh? Awww don't cry. You were his dream come true."

At that instant, she knew what she would name their daughter. "Dream. Your name is Dream. You are your Daddy's Dream."

Tricia, who was in the other room had heard a loud crying. She ran inside her goddaughter's room and saw her friend crying a river.

"I miss Michael."

BOOK TWO

DREAM LOVED when her birthday came around. That meant nothing but birthday presents galore. In one week, she would be 20 years old and one year away from the big 21, which meant that she could legally get into clubs. No longer would she have to sneak in clubs or use fake IDs. She couldn't wait!

"So what are you doing for your birthday, Dream?" asked her best friend, Tanya.

"I don't know yet. I haven't thought about it."

"Bitch, please!" Tanya shouted. "Your birthday is next fucking week and you don't know what you wanna do? I can't believe what I just heard."

"For real, Tanya. I don't have anything planned. Shit, I have had parties, so I don't want one of those. I just don't know what I wanna do."

"You serious, ain't you? Wow this is a first, you usually have shit planned six months early."

"Tell me about it."

"What's up with Jamal? He not taking you out or nothing?"

"Fuck Jamal!"

"Damn, what happened with y'all."

"All he does is stay in the street, and every time I call him to come over, he's too busy."

"Well shit, Dream. You know what he does. That's why he's in the street."

"Yea, and what's that supposed to mean? He can at least come spend time with me. He probably got some other bitch out there."

"Well, you know how them niggas are, and he got a Beemer, so yea, he could be showboating some other scank around, who knows.
"

"And you know something else, Tanya? I'm tired of messing with street dudes. Jamal got a good education and he's out there fucking up with that shit. What if he gets shot or goes to jail. Where is that gonna leave me."

"Yea, I feel you girl."

"That's another reason why I say 'fuck Jamal'."

"But you know, as soon as that nigga come around, all that shit you talking is going straight out the window."

"Yea, well I'm just saying I'm getting fed up with the bullshit."

"Anyway, let me go home girl. I gotta go and fucking babysit my little sister again. My fucking mother is gonna start paying me. She's always running out with her new man and shit. Fuck, my pussy gets wet too. I could be out getting my freak on."

They both busted out laughing. "Anyway, call me and let me know what's up with your b-day."

"Aight Tanya. Drive safe. You know how them niggas on the road are."

"Girl, I got this. Later."

"Later," Dream replied.

Dream and Tanya had been friends since junior high school. They had met by Tanya jumping in when two girls tried to jump Dream. Tanya didn't like the other girls anyway, so she helped Dream beat the girls up. Everybody in the school either loved or hated Dream. The boys loved her because she was so goddamned pretty with an Indian beauty, and everybody wanted to date her. The girls on the other hand were so jealous of her that they would pick fights with her, which she would win.

"Don't let the good looks fool y'all, 'cause I'll whip your ass," she would tell them.

But Tanya was just as pretty as Dream and besides, she thought Dream had some spirit about herself, that she was cool and down to earth. So after they beat the girls up, they had become the best of friends. They were like sisters.

Dream sat in her room wondering if she should call Jamal. She picked up her cell phone and pushed the speed dial button to Jamal's number.

"What up, who dis?" Jamal asked into his phone without looking at it.

"Fuck, you mean who dis? You got caller ID, nigga."

"Oh shit, Dream. I didn't even look at my phone. I just answered it."

"Whatever. Anyway, I called to ask you what we doing for my birthday next week.

Jamal, who was busy getting his dick sucked by some chick he had just met, said, "Damn baby. I gotta go away next week on some business shit."

"You always gotta do something when it comes to me, Jamal."

"Come on, baby. Don't be like that. When I get back we'll celebrate your birthday then."

"Don't bother. And fuck you Jamal." And she hung up the phone. She waited to see if he would call back. If he did, that meant he gave a fuck. If he didn't, it was over. He never did.

Dream went downstairs where her mother was in the kitchen cooking.

"What's wrong with you?" Jasmine asked.

"I hate boys. They always thinking about themselves."

"That's why you should just focus on school and finish. Then you can concentrate on boys if you choose to."

"You know what, Ma? You right."

"I know I'm right."

"I'm gonna finish school first, then I'm gonna become a lesbian."

"What??" Dream could not stop laughing.

"You should have seen your face, Ma. You almost jumped out of your skin."

"Girl, that's not funny. Don't play like that."

"Ma, yuck. You think I would go that way? Please I'm strictly d... oops. I mean, I like boys."

"Well, you better stay liking boys or I'll disown you."

"For real, Ma?"

"In a heartbeat."

"Well you ain't gotta worry 'bout that 'cause I'mma forever be straight," Dream said. "Ma, what was Daddy like?"

Jasmine had not expected that. She was caught off guard. "Your father?" she said surprised. "Let me see. Your father was a prince. My prince. He was so handsome and charming and boy could he sing. I fell in love with him the first time we met."

"He did look good. I be looking at the pictures with all those superstars. Wow he was big time."

"Yep, your father was certainly up there with the big people."

"Did they put that drunk driver in jail who crashed into him?"

"I can't recall," Jasmine lied.

Jasmine had told her daughter that her father had died in a car accident because she did not want her to know that her father had been shot and killed by some low life called Stacks who was still doing time. She had saw in her daughter's eyes a vengeful spirit and she did not want her to be seeking revenge on her father's murderer. So she just lied and said he was in a car accident.

"I wish I could have met him, if only once," Dream said in a low voice. "I know he would have loved me."

"Of course," Jasmine said. "He was thrilled when I was pregnant with you. When I told him, he asked me to marry him on the spot."

"Aww. So Daddy was romantic too?"

128

"Yep."

"Why did they call him Daddy?"

"That was what they called him before we met. Oh!" The doorbell rang just then. Dream ran to answer it.

"G-Daddy!" which was short for god daddy.

"What's up, Little Princess?" Peanuts said. He handed her a long box with a ribbon on it. "Happy Birthday."

"Whew G-daddy, what is it?"

"Open it." She saw the box and saw a diamond necklace that must have cost at least three grand.

"Whew, it's pretty," Dream screamed. "Ma, look what G-daddy got me!"

Peanuts walked inside and kissed Jasmine and hugged her.

"Now what have you bought that child now?"

"Oh just a little something for her b-day."

Dream ran upstairs to call Tanya and tell her, but not before she jumped up on Peanuts and kissed him and thanked him over and over again.

"You gotta stop spoiling her like that. That girl is gonna be rotten."

"She deserves it. She's a good kid."

"Yea, but that necklace, I know, cost a lot."

"A couple grand, it's nothing. But anyway, how you doing these days?"

"I'm good."

"Look I wanna really say sorry about what happened last month. I lost control, I ..."

"It's fine. We're good. Just don't do it anymore."

"You got that." Peanuts had come on so strong to Jasmine that he lost his cool. Ever since Daddy had introduced Jasmine to Peanuts, he had wanted her.

"It's just that I'm feeling you, Jasmine. I always have. What's wrong with us going out?"

"You know we can't do that, Peanuts. I mean, how would that look? Michael was your best friend."

"Yea, but he would have wanted you to move on, and who better would take his place than me?"

"Peanuts look how you sound."

"How do I sound?"

"We are family, Peanuts. You're Dream's godfather, for crying out loud and she loves you as that, and I love you for a very close friend and nothing more."

Just then, Dream came downstairs and she was singing. Peanuts heard her and could not believe his ears.

"Aye yo. Do you hear her?" Peanuts shouted with excitement.

"Ya, I hear her."

"Why didn't you tell me Dream could sing like that?"

"Cause I want my child to be a lawyer, not a singer."

"C'mon, Jasmine, why you being so selfish?"

"Listen, I don't want to lose somebody else because of their fame, or whatever. I can't take any more of that."

"You know I have been looking for a female singer all this time and..."

"What y'all talking about?" Dream interrupted.

"Where did you get that voice, Little Princess? You sounding like you need to be on a record."

Dream started blushing to the question and compliment her G-daddy had given her. The child had a phenomenal voice. The kind that if a producer had heard her sing would instantly want to work with her. Such as her G-daddy, who had a recording studio called Peanuts Productions, of course, funded by his boss, Luis Sanchez.

But Dream paid her voice no mind. She never once thought about singing for other people. She just loved singing. Even though her father had been a superstar, she herself would become a lawyer. She was intrigued by helping criminals get off. So singing never crossed her mind. Until now.

"Listen, why don't you just come by the studio? You know where it is. So some people I know could at least just hear you, please?"

"I don't know, G-daddy. Me singing in front of other people? I …"

"You will do just fine, don't worry. It will be alright. Watch, you'll see."

Dream looked at her mother, "Ma?"

"C'mon Jasmine, please?" Peanuts begged.

"Listen, Peanuts. If it's going to interfere with her school work…"

"It won't. I just want them to hear her. That's all."

"Well, Ma?" Dream always respected her mother's decision.

"Just to let them hear you nothing more. Jasmine you won't regret this," an excited Peanuts said.

But deep down, Jasmine knew she had made the wrong decision. She knew her daughter was super talented and whoever heard her would instantly want to sign her up. Like her father. That's why she never told Peanuts or any of her contacts. Yep, she had definitely made a mistake.

Peanuts sat in his plush leather chair at his recording studio overlooking Manhattan. His office was on the 72nd floor, so the view was spectacular. He sat there in heavy thought, reflecting back on it all. The drug business had been good to him. He had made so much money that he had to get an offshore account. Luis Sanchez had put him on to that. Money was not all he had made though. He had his share of enemies that he had made, as well. Other drug rivals who were out to get his turf because of the flow of money it was bringing in. He dealt with them swiftly. He was too powerful. Now he was CEO at a thriving music business called Peanuts Productions that had some of the top stars in the business on its labels. His chance came at the gathering of his friend Daddy's funeral 20 years back when Jasmine had introduced him to some very influential people. They saw money in him and he saw opportunity in them, whereas he could wash his money.

His thoughts were interrupted when a female came into his office. She was sexy as always wearing a very expensive Gucci outfit and a necklace with a matching tennis bracelet that must have cost close to two hundred thousand dollars.

"What's up, Mr. Businessman?" Cindy said.

"Yo, what up Cin?"

They had not seen each other in a few months, but they still did business together through other contacts. Cindy was busy herself maintaining three beauty salons and her own strip club. She had certainly come up.

"So you still doing the music thing I see."

"Yep still doing it."

"Nice office you got here, I see you upgraded."

"Yea, I had a few items imported from Paris to give me an eccentric look," he bragged. "Why, you like?"

"It's tasteful," Cindy shot back.

"Guess who I'm gonna have on my label singing for me."

"Who?" she asked.

"Daddy's daughter, Dream."

Cindy didn't seem to be impressed. She looked at him with an upside down smile and said, "Really. I didn't know that you was still messing around with his family. And I know the only reason that you're godfather to his daughter is to get close to that bitch, Jasmine."

"See, there you go with the bullshit. Do I detect a hint of jealousy?"

"Whatever. Look, I came here to see you and to talk to you about some business that would be good for both of us."

"Aww shit. Here we go."

"Peanuts, this is serious," she shouted.

"Aight, aight. Damn, what's up?"

"Some people I know got some pure ass coke for a very nice price that is much cheaper than what you're getting it for and the coke is off the chain."

"And how do you know that it's off the chain?"

"My people tested it out. They say they never had nothing like it before and if we had it our percentage will triple what we are making now."

"I don't know, Cin. I've been with my source for a while and I can't see myself going behind his back and ..."

He was cut off. "Peanuts, please. It's time to go out on your own. You've made that Sanchez cat over 5 hundred million, maybe more and you deserve to be boss."

Cindy had a point, he thought to himself. He did make Luis Sanchez richer while he only had a few mill tucked away, he wasn't as rich as he wanted to be. And he wanted more power.

"So, how good do you know these people?" Cindy smiled, knowing that she had won his attention on the subject.

"Very well. And please don't worry about Sanchez. These people are way more powerful than him. If we deal with them, we could get rid of Sanchez, with no problem. "

Peanuts just sat in thought, wondering where he was going with this, not knowing that every word was heard through a tiny bug hidden within the walls of his studio.

Luis Sanchez was born in the Dominican Republic. His father was in the oil business, so he had been rich from the very beginning. He was a scrawny little boy who stayed underneath his mother most of the time. The boys in his community had picked on him and called him a mama's boy. But in spite of the outbursts, he stayed underneath his mother all the time anyway. He loved her. She was his protection. His father was always away on business so he had nobody else that would pay attention to him. He was not interested in girls, so that put another label on him. A fag. Still the words that the other kids spoke out at him didn't get to him. They were all jealous that their family wasn't as rich as his.

"Don't worry about what anybody calls you," his mother would say.

And he didn't. He felt that he was different from all the other kids. Much smarter. The teachers at his school were impressed by how quick he mastered every subject with a speed that was not normal for a 10-year-old. So he was advanced to three higher grades. Luiz Sanchez loved studying. He always asked questions that sometimes his mother could not even answer. However, given that she was not an educated woman, his father had taught him everything. Astrology, history, mathematics. He even gave him some lessons on how to run the family business. Yep. Luis Sanchez was very much different than other kids. When they were playing, he was loaning. One day, while his mother, who was beautiful just like a flower and polite as she wanna be, was followed by some local drug peddlers. She was opening the door to their home and was rushed by two of the followers.

"Shh. If you make one sound, I'll kill you on the spot."

Young Luis Sanchez came running out when he heard his mother entering and stopped short when he saw his mother pinned down on the floor by these punks.

"Mommy," he shouted.

"Luis, run! Run, Luis!" she screamed.

He tried but another one of the followers caught him.

"Hey you little punk. Where do you think you're going? You're gonna stay here and watch the show. Do you hear what I say, Padre?"

"I'm going first," one of them said. He jumped on Luiz's mother and started ripping her skirt away. Luis Sanchez could not bear to look at his mother get raped. He closed his eyes, but the sounds and screams of his mother had invaded his ears. The punks had taken turns in raping his mother brutally. She laid there traumatized. And as if that wasn't enough, they took some cocaine and stuffed it inside her, then they took a needle and injected some more cocaine inside her.

"Now Padre. Look at your mother. See how much of a whore she is, as well as a junkie."

They got themselves together and ran out of the house leaving a crying Luis Sanchez behind. He knelt down to his mother and tried his best to talk to her. But her lifeless body would not respond. With a combination of the drugs inside her and the shock of being raped, she died right there in their house. Luis Sanchez would never be the same. His father, who had a weak heart already had died of a heart attack, as soon as he heard the news of his wife. Luis Sanchez, at 10 years old, was alone.

On his 18th birthday, he inherited five million dollars, as well as his father's business, which was being run by his father's lawyer over the years until Luis was old enough to take it over. Well, much to his surprise, Sanchez was much smarter than he thought when he went up against his father's investors. When they tried to swindle the business from him, thinking he was just a boy and didn't know anything about the oil business, he outsmarted them all. Over the years, he would double his earnings in the business, making it more profitable than his father had. He was becoming a powerful man. As well as his money, his knowledge on all subjects had advanced. Technology seemed to be his best subject. He also dove into law and politics. He had women, but no wife. He didn't wanna get caught up into feelings because he thought of that as being weak. Vivid images would sometimes parade his thoughts of his mother's death and they would not go away. One day, he had a thought on how to rid these images once and for all. Revenge! He had revisited his old neighborhood to learn the whereabouts of his mother's murderers. He had remembered that they belonged to a gang called the young Tigers. As if the Gods had blessed him, the young Tigers still existed in the very neighborhood, which he grew up in. Sanchez had hired some men to kidnap the three punks who were not that much older than he was. The three punks who thought they were tough were brought to Sanchez's old house. The same house his mother died in. The same house they would die in.

"You do not remember me huh, Padre?"

"Who the fuck are you mister. We have no business with you."

"Aww, but Padre you do have business with me. Today I want all three of you to get rid of some pure cocaine for me. A kilo to be exact."

"We can't sell all of that in no one day," one of them shouted.

"I didn't say sell, Padre. I said get rid of."

"What da fuck are you saying man?" the man said, getting irritated and tired of word games.

"Today each of you is going to eat these three kilos of cocaine."

"What?" they shouted. "You must be stupid man. We not doing no shit like that. What are you, crazy?"

Just then, Sanchez ordered his men to bring their mothers and wives, who was tied up and gagged in the back room, up where they were. The men all looked at their families with a frightened stare.

"Aye yo man what da fuck…"

"Now, Padre. Listen to me very careful so that your family can live. You three are going to eat this cocaine slowly ounce by ounce. Comprende?"

"Why the fuck are you doing this?"

Sanchez smiled and said, "If you really don't remember me, let me make you remember. Years ago in this very house, you three raped and put drugs up inside one who was very dear to me. You stole my family. And today, you are going to pay for your crimes."

"You are insane, Mister."

"Yes, I am. Now start eating or a piece of each one of your family members is going to come off of their body."

They had no choice; they were cornered. They didn't want to see their loved ones hurt, so they ate ounce by ounce of the raw pure cocaine until you saw nothing but white foam and blood mixed racing from their eyes, nose and mouth. They died right there.

Yes, he was a monster, but a rich, smart and powerful one. He had moved to America, selling his product and expanding his business. He didn't care who he was selling his product to, just as long as it was getting sold. The officials were on to him, but were not smart in trapping him. He was way ahead of them. He had people in high places that were within his circle. They couldn't touch him, though they had tried many times over. Sanchez loved the cat and mouse game because he knew that he could win.

Why do these people think that they can outfox me? He said to himself. He felt that no one was smarter than he. That's why he couldn't believe what he had heard on his recorder.

"So Peanuts and that slimy bitch think that they are smarter than me?" he said to no one. "We will see who gets rid of whom."

Inside of his safe was some information on a tape, (CD). Information that would destroy these two birds he thought. Yes. It was time that this information be used. See how precious gifts come in handy.

❀   ❀   ❀

DREAM PULLED up in front of Peanuts' Productions in her baby blue beamer. She looked as if she belonged in Hollywood somewhere 'cause she looked like money. Her mother was chief editor of a newspaper and was always in demand. Plus, the royalties were always coming in from her father's music. So Dream was sitting pretty well. She walked into her godfather's office where he was sitting in his expensive leather chair.

"Hey G-Daddy."

"Dream!" he shouted back. "So glad that you're here. I was just talking 'bout you."

"This office is bangin' G-Daddy. What happened? You did it over or something?"

"Yea, I renovated the whole office. Nice, ain't it?"

"You got good taste."

"Thanks goddaughter. Well, are you ready to hit those notes?"

"I guess so. I'm a little nervous though."

"Like I said, you'll be fine. You only gonna be singing for me and a few others, don't worry."

"Okay. So where they at?"

"C'mon."

They walked out of Peanuts' office and got on the elevator and took it downstairs to the studio. When Dream came out of the elevator and saw all the state of the art equipment, she got more nervous, but was in awe at all of the high tech stuff.

"Wow, G-Daddy! This is nice."

"I know, right? This is a million dollar studio here. We record a lot of music out of here. Some big names come through here to do their thang."

"So you just did the whole building over huh?"

"Well, not the whole building," he chuckled.

Three men walked out of another room.

"Aye. You must be Dream. I have heard a lot about you. Used to work with your father on some things. It's a pleasure to meet you."

"Nice to meet you, too," she smiled shaking the man's beefy hand

"Peanuts tells me that you've got one helluva voice."

"It's okay, I guess."

"Well, if you're Daddy's daughter, it's gotta run in the family, and if it does, you got it because your father had a voice that was out of this world!"

"So, Dream. You ready?" Peanuts jumped in.

"Yea," she said nervously.

"Okay, do you think you can sing this song by Selena Jordan?"

"Yes."

"Okay, so give it your best, and remember you'll be fine."

Dream was out of this world nervous. She never sang in front of people that she didn't know, let alone in front of a mike. But when she got her groove, there was no stopping her. The girl had pipes on her that were remarkable. The manager could not believe his ears were hearing something so beautiful. Dream was hitting note after note.

"Hold up!" the man with the beefy hands shouted.

Dream was confused. "Did I mess up?"

"Did she mess up?" the man said under his breath. "Of course you messed up... By not coming here sooner! Young lady you are sensational!"

"I told you!" Peanuts shouted out.

"I am?" Dream asked.

"Yes you are!" he said. "When can we get her a contract?"

"Well technically, I told her mother that I would just let you hear her."

"Peanuts, what are you saying. Are you telling me that she can't sing for us?"

"I can handle her mother."

"Well you better 'cause I want her. This girl can sing. And she's Daddy's daughter. She'll be an instant hit."

"Dream was standing there soaking all of this up. All kinds of feelings were going through her. She didn't realize that she would become a star, but she was headed that way.

❀   ❀   ❀

KAREEM JACKSON was one helluva basketball player. He was drafted by the Detroit Pistons after a four-year college tenure at Georgetown, of which he helped win a final four championship. Even today he is one of the top players in the league. He was given a scholarship to go to college after a scout had witnessed his skills in high school, but if he had not had that scholarship, he still would have been able to go to any school he desired. Daddy had seen to that before his death. That was one thing that Daddy did was give back to the community.

Kareem loved Daddy like he was his biological father. He was so hurt of the passing of his mentor that he couldn't eat or sleep. He cried for days. Jasmine knew how much her husband cherished his hobby: Being with the boys at the club. And she also knew that Kareem was special to him. So, she made sure that she stayed involved with the Boys Club and especially Kareem.

"Kareem, I want you to know you are always welcome to my home," she had told him.

"Thank you, Mrs. Flowers." And from that day up until now, he had been like family. Jasmine and Dream always had the best seats to his games wherever the game was played. Dream loved her god-brother, in fact, she adored him. She had her secret fantasies about him, but that's all they were, was fantasies. She would always tease him about marrying him, but he would just blow her off.

"We gonna get married, right Kareem? And have a big wedding?"

"Girl, quit playing. You like a sister to me, Dream."

"So? You not my real brother."

"I'm brother enough, so stop playin'."

"I hate you," she said smiling.

She was 16 then, and he 28. And they loved each other. Kareem would do anything for Dream, just like Daddy did for him. He would always be there for her.

Dream was ecstatic and excited by her godfather and his team wanting her to sing for them. She had never thought of herself singing professionally. Now she was asked to be on a label. She had to tell someone. She called her best friend, but got the answering machine.

"Tanya, this is Dream. I'm on my way home. Call me back or meet me there. I gotta tell you something, girl. Bye!"

She hung up the phone and couldn't keep from smiling. She thought to herself, "Damn! All the people I could meet in the music business!"

"She was gonna be a star like her father," she said to herself. But she had no clue what she was getting into or with whom.

❀ ❀ ❀

PEANUTS DROVE his convertible Aston Martin out of the garage of Peanuts Productions. It was a gift that was given to him by Luis Sanchez. The automobile was a luxury that any exotic car lover would die for. Its color was navy blue with a peach interior. Twenty-inch rims and of course, it was bullet proof. With one touch of the button, the convertible would instantly cover the roof. But like all gifts from Sanchez, the Aston Martin had a recording device hidden inside the built-in navigation system. Peanuts was smiling as he sped down a Manhattan street. Everything was going good for him. He had money and a life that was filled with rich opportunities. His goddaughter Dream would make him richer than he had ever been. Her voice was fresh and young. The music business needed a new lady and he had it right in the palm of his hand. Just maybe by making Dream an overnight success, Jasmine would take to him. He still fantasized about having her. He still wanted her, to be inside her. At times, when he had sex with other women including his longtime girlfriend Shay-Shay, he would think of Jasmine, picture her as he would ejaculate. He pulled up in front of a Manhattan penthouse, and got out of the Aston with a silver suitcase. The valet parking attendant took the car and parked it. Peanuts went inside the building and pressed the elevator button to the top floor. Luis Sanchez was in his chair, waiting for him.

"Peanuts, my boy. Come in, come in. Have a seat," Sanchez said.

"Damn, Sanchez. You got this place hooked up real nice."

"Oh, this old place. It's nothing compared to the one I have in Florida. Anyway, look at you. You look a little better since the last time I saw you. You seemed a bit stressed."

"Yea, well things are looking up these days. Here's your suitcase."

Sanchez took the suitcase which contained half a million dollars, and placed it under his desk.

"Looking up, you say?"

"Yea, with the music business. I got some new prospects lined up."

"Oh. I see, I see! So how is the other business going? Are you having any thoughts about stepping down from it?" Sanchez asked.

Peanuts was caught off guard with the question. "No, but what makes you ask that question?"

"I mean, look at you. You have a thriving studio and production thing going on. That's bringing you good money in. I'm quite sure you've thought about going legit."

"Well, it has crossed my mind a couple of times."

"So why haven't you brought it up, if it crossed your mind?"

"I mean, it wasn't no big issue. It just was a thought. Besides, I love what I do out there in those streets."

"Tell you what, give it another six months, then all of our street affairs are done. I'll have Lopez take over Brooklyn, whereas I will still have contacts in that borough."

Peanuts could not believe what he was just told. He didn't expect to be dealt such a blow. And all he could do was just sit there and take it 'cause he knew Sanchez meant every word of it. Besides he had plans of his own that would still include him keeping Brooklyn.

❀ ❀ ❀

DREAM PULLED up to her house and saw that her friend Tanya was there waiting on her. She couldn't wait to tell her the news.

"Girl, where have you been? I've been calling your phone off the hook!" an elevated Dream said.

"I lost my phone. I paid too much money for that damn phone and now it's lost. I got your message when I checked my voicemail, so I just came on over. It sounded like you hit the lottery or something."

"Close, but not that."

"So, what then? What happened? Tell me! My ears are ringing!"

"Girl, I got a record deal!"

"Bitch, you lying! For real? When? With who?"

"With my godfather. I went to his studio today to let some of his people hear me and they signed me on the spot."

"Wow! My best friend is gonna blow up! I've been telling yo ass all along to sing for somebody. I'm glad yo godfather got you hooked up because girl, you can blow!"

"I'm so nervous and happy, I don't know what to do!"

"Girl, if I was in your shoes, that's all I'd be thinking about is shoes!"

"What? Shoes?" Dream said.

"Yep. Shoes, clothes, jewelry, you name it!"

They both enjoyed a good laugh.

"There'll be plenty of time for that. And you know you my girl, so wherever I go, you go."

"Wow, just think of all the people you gonna meet. They gonna wanna hook up with you to do songs and shit. Girl, you gonna be a hit!"

"I know, there are so many people I do wanna meet. I probably wouldn't know how to act."

"And I'm gonna be right there with you, not knowing how to act."

"Let's go tell my mother the news."

"Ma! Ma! Guess what!" an excited Dream yelled.

"What? You got a record deal?"

"That's not fair! How did you know?"

"If you could see the look in your eyes. You look just like your father when he got his."

"Hello, Mrs. Flowers."

"Hello, Tanya. And how are you doing?"

"Fine, ain't it kool that she's gonna be a star?"

"Yes, it's kool."

"Ma, I'm so excited I don't know what to do."

"So what are you gonna do about school, Dream?"

"Oh boy, here it comes," Dream said.

"Well your education is important, Dream, and I put up a lot of money for your education."

"I could pay you back."

"That's not the point. Money is not the issue here. Your education is."

"But she could go part time, Mrs. Flowers. She still could get her education. A lot of celebrities do."

"Oh really? Name them."

"Uh. Uh, shoot, what's her name?" Tanya was tongue stuck. She couldn't think of anyone that was on the road all the time who still had time for school.

"Well, I can't think of nobody off hand, but there is…," Tanya said.

"Oh Ma, please let me do this, please!"

Jasmine thought for a second. She didn't want to let her daughter go out there in that world, but how could she deprive her of the life she seemed destined for. Her voice was for sure a gift that the world would accept immediately.

"Okay, okay, but we are still gonna try and squeeze some education in there somehow."

Dream jumped on her mother and kissed her all over.

"Oh thank you, Ma! You the best mommy anyone could have!"

Dream and Tanya went up to her room to make preparations.

The game was the same all over. It had both its pros and cons.

"Dream, you gonna be the shit with all the people you gonna meet. Girl, I'm talking about fashion, to making videos. Aww, man! My best friend is a superstar."

"But just remember, wherever I go, you going with me."

"What you gonna do 'bout Jamal. Girl when he finds out that you got a record deal, he gonna wanna marry you and shit."

"Fuck Jamal, all he wanna do is stay in them streets. He not gonna give a damn about me singing."

"Are you crazy? His girl gonna be selling records, and you think he not gonna care? Please. That boy gonna wanna be in the videos and stop acting like you don't love that nigga, 'cause you do."

"I know right. I love the fuck outta him, but he not doing me right and I don't have time for his shit no more."

"Well once he finds out about this, trust. He'll act right. And if not, shit, look at all those fine ass rappers. They gonna want you."

"I want Jamal," Dream said.

Meanwhile, a deal was going down on the other side of town. The man in the black Beamer had promised himself this would be the last drug deal hustle he would do if all went well. And he had every right to want to quit 'cause this was a million dollar deal. However, the same thing was going on in the mind of the man who was sitting in his jeep, holding a shotgun watching the whole thing. A white Jaguar pulled up next to the Beamer. A Latino man got out holding a briefcase and got into the Beamer. They exchanged pleasantries as well as briefcases and the deal was done.

But before either one of them noticed the man with the mask on, the shotgun exploded, pumping two large holes in both bodies. Death was instant. The masked man took both briefcases and jumped up to the jeep he was sitting in earlier. The jeep sped off leaving behind two dead bodies, one by the name of Carlos Santana, and one by the name of Jamal James.

"I'm gonna call my baby now and tell him the good news. I wanna hear how excited he gonna be when I tell him."

Dream was calling Jamal's number, but he wasn't picking up. As usual, when he didn't answer his phone, she thought that he was playing her. But when breaking news came across the television mentioning two murders and she saw that one of them was Jamal as his picture came across the screen, she know then why he wasn't answering his phone. Jamal was dead.

"Oh my God!" Tanya cried out!

Dream busted out crying, as the newsman finished describing the story.

This was supposed to be a special birthday. Dream should have been celebrating her birthday and her being signed with a recording label. Instead, she was preparing for her boyfriend's funeral. She did not understand how something good and bad could happen at the same time. She attended Jamal's funeral accompanied by her friend, Tanya. Tanya was there for her friend at the time she really needed someone. It was a crowded affair. A whole lot of people came out to see him off, including his other girl with their son who looked just like Jamal. Dream was stunned. She did not know he had a family. *Oh, well,* she thought. *He's gone now. No use getting mad and stressed out. Nobody has him.*

This was like a brand new beginning. She would focus on her music career with her G-Daddy. There was nothing else to think about but that. He had given her a couple of songs to go home and get familiar with. Just to practice her vocals. And she would do just that. Not knowing that one of those songs was a critical part of history.

Jasmine was hearing things, but the things that she was hearing she shouldn't be hearing, as in her bedroom singing a song that she had gotten from her G-Daddy along with a couple of others.

The very same song that her daughter was singing was sung to her 20 years ago. But how could that be? Suddenly memories came rushing back to her on the night that Daddy sang it to her. He had told her she inspired him to write that song and he was going to record it the next day. That was the day he had been killed. So the song never got recorded and he had taken his backpack with him where he kept his songs, but that was never found. Now their daughter 20 years later was singing the lyrics to that song.

"Oh, Ma! You shocked me!" Dream told her mother.

"Sorry," she said. "Baby, that's a nice song. Where did you get that from?"

"Oh this song? G-Daddy told me to rehearse this. He thinks that it could be a single. It sounds nice, right? Whoever wrote this was good."

Was good, Jasmine thought to herself.

"Yes, it sounds really good. I heard you all the way from the kitchen."

"I didn't know I was that loud."

"Yes, you were loud, but you sound so wonderful. So you sure this is what you want to do?"

"Oh yes, Mommy. I want to sing, just like my Daddy."

Jasmine saw in her daughter's eyes happiness and excitement, but something was wrong with this whole thing. How did Peanuts have access to her late husband's songs? Unless...

"Oh My God!" she said to herself. She had to go pay him a visit.

Jasmine walked into the office of Peanuts and took a seat. She never had been here and was surprised at how beautiful Peanuts' office/studio was. Peanuts walked toward Jasmine gave her a kiss and hugged her, glad and surprised that she was here. She had called him and said that she wanted to talk to him, but she wanted to come there. He wondered what was so important. He hoped it wasn't about Dream and the contract. And he hoped that she had changed her mind about being with him.

"Jasmine, what a surprise. What's up? What brings you here?"

"I came here to ask you about the song you gave Dream to sing."

"Hot song, right? You like it?"

"Yea, I like it. It's a very nice song. Where did you get if from?"

"One of my staff wrote it. I think it fits Dream. She hits every note the way it's supposed to be sung."

"Peanuts, your staff didn't write that song."

"What are you talking about?"

"Michael wrote that song for me, the day before he got killed, and nobody ever heard it before. So tell me again, Peanuts. Where did you get that song?"

Peanuts was stuck and lost for words.

"Jasmine, I haven't the slightest idea what you're talking about."

"There was a backpack, in which Michael always carried his songs with him to the studio. I asked his manager what happened to it that night. He told me that he left with it, and I don't think he would lie, because Michael never left his material anyplace. He always took it with him. But the police said they saw no backpack. So again. How did you get that song?!"

"Jasmine, why are you doing this? Where are you going with this?"

"All I want to know is how did you get that song?"

"C'mon Jasmine."

"Peanuts, did you have anything to do with Michael getting robbed? Were you after those songs?"

"Are you crazy or something? Why would I be behind my friend's death?"

"That's a good question. So if you won't tell me where you got that song, I'll find out on my own. And please stay away from me and my daughter. You can forget about her singing for you."

Jasmine got up and walked out of the office. As she was walking out, Cindy came in from the other door.

"Well, well. I see that you had a vision."

"Yea."

"You know she has to go, right?"

"What do you mean, 'Go'?" Peanuts asked.

"Don't get stupid on me now. You know exactly what I mean"

"You ain't tired of killing or letting people die?"

"I'm just saying, she knows too much and she is pointing fingers. Why would you give the daughter of Daddy a song that was stolen from him to sing?"

"I didn't know that was his song. Must have gotten it mixed up with the others."

"Well we don't know if she has a copy of that song or not. And she seems pretty bent on finding out what's going on. So, she must die."

Peanuts just stared into the ceiling, wondering where this was going.

Jasmine was fuming. All kinds of emotions were running through her.

How could a friend harm a friend? She asked herself.

She was certain that Peanuts was behind her husband's death, but how was she going to prove it. With all the thoughts running through her mind, she did not notice a black Ford 150 truck that had been following her. Suddenly, the truck picked up speed and rammed into the back of her. Jasmine was in a state of shock as the force of the truck took her off her guard. She was scared for her life as the F150 rammed her car again. Instantly, she knew the driver was deliberately trying to run her off the road. She tried to speed up away from the truck, but driving her car faster made it harder to steer as her pursuer kept up with her, ramming her off the road. Jasmine's care flipped over several times. The driver of the F150 sped past, knowing that the intended accident had been successful. An onlooker had witnessed Jasmine's car being run off the road and being flipped over. He raced toward her car before an explosion went off. He saw Jasmine upside down. She was still moving a little bit. With speed and carefulness, he pulled jasmine out. She was still breathing, but short breaths. He took out his cell phone and called a number.

"This is Dr. Jones. I need a paramedic at Tyler Lane. Quickly! A woman has been in a car accident."

"It's gonna be okay. Hold on Miss," Dr. Jones said to a bewildered Jasmine.

Dream's world was falling to pieces. First, her boyfriend Jamal had been shot and killed during a bad drug deal. Even though she had broken off from him, she cared for him greatly. He was her first and only boyfriend. So she cried for two days after hearing the news. And now her mother was in a hospital because of a car accident. The person that had saved her from the car had been a doctor and he was the one who took care of her. He said that she only suffered some minor bruises and a broken hip, but she would recover in weeks. He also had mentioned that he witnessed the other car was deliberately trying to knock her off the road. He said the driver was a female, but he couldn't get the license plate number. Dream was crying all over the place. Home alone, she was a mess. Her best friend Tanya was in North Carolina with her grandparents and said that she would be home in three days. She needed somebody right now, someone who she could talk to. She called Kareem.

"Hello, Kareem?"

"Wassup Dreamy?"

"Mama was in a car accident," she told him, sniffling on the phone.

"What? When?"

"Yesterday. I tried to call you, but kept getting the machine and I didn't want to leave a message like that on your voicemail."

"I'm coming home tomorrow," he said. "I'll take the early flight out first thing in the morning. Are you okay?" he asked.

"I'm fine, but I'm just scared and lonely."

"Don't worry. She will be fine."

"I know."

"And you just be easy."

"Okay, I will."

"Dreamy, I love you."

"Me too, Reem."

She hung up the phone. She could always count on him and she knew that he would be here as soon as he could. She couldn't wait. She needed somebody. With nothing to do, she went snooping around her mother's things, looking at old photos of her mother and father. There were pictures that she hadn't ever seen before. She was looking at them, smiling and crying at the same time. Something was back in her mother's closet, another box that she had never seen before. She took it out and looked inside of it. There she came across her parents' marriage license and photos of them getting married. But underneath the pile was a newspaper clipping. Reading the headlines, she could not believe her eyes. It read "Rising R&B singer Michael "Daddy" Flowers shot and killed during a robbery."

The headlines didn't mention anything about a car accident. Dream was puzzled.

Why did her mother tell her that her father was killed in a car accident? She thought to herself.

She read the whole article over and over again. Crying and hurt all over again, as if this had just happened. The article also had who was behind the killing of her father: Damian "Stacks" Jones, who was doing time upstate New York at the Sing-Sing Corrections. Dream wondered was he still in jail. She would make a call, and if he was, she would pay him a visit.

Dream had never been to visit anyone in prison before. So she was a little nervous. She asked herself was she doing the right thing. Why did she feel so compelled to confront her father's murderer? What kind of questions would she ask him? What answers was she looking for? And when she got them, what good would it do to her. She would soon find out.

Usuf Akbar walked in the visiting room, surprised to have a visitor when it had been several years since he'd had one. The guard pointed to the booth where Dream awaited him. Usuf walked toward the booth seeing a beautiful young lady who he had never seen before. He sat down with a bewildered look on his face.

153

"Do we know each other?" he asked.

Sitting in front of Dream was the man accused of killing her father. He was handsome. He wore a Kufi and had muscles popping out everywhere. He looked refined and regal and very righteous.

"Was this the man who killed my father?" she asked herself.

"Humm my name is Dream Flowers. Are you who they call Stacks?"

"I went by that name a very long time ago. My name is Usuf Akbar and how may I help you?"

Dream didn't know where to begin or how. So she just came out with it.

"Hmmm, the reason I'm here, the reason I came to see you is to ask you why did you kill my father."

A stunned Usuf said, "Excuse me. I beg your pardon!"

"My father, Michael 'Daddy' Flowers. Why did you kill him? Why did you rob me of someone I didn't get a chance to know?"

Usuf sat back in his chair and just stared at this beautiful young lady, who had struck a nerve. At the corner of his mouth came a little smile before he began his response.

"So you are the daughter of Daddy, huh? I remember so well about that situation and it is rather surprising to me that a beautiful young lady would appear from nowhere after twenty years to ask me that question. Yes, me and your father had some beef. He broke my nose. I promised to kill him. He became a superstar, and I backed off."

"Backed off?" Dream asked.

"Yes, I couldn't be involved in a murder like that. He had everything going for him with that music thang. Hell, I even bought some of his music. So I couldn't murder an R&B singer."

"I don't understand. So if you didn't kill my father, then who did, and why are you in here for that?"

154

"Those are both good questions. The gun that was in my house was said to be the murder weapon. To this day, I still don't know for sure how it all happened, but I do know, that bitch Cindy was behind it all. She was in my house that night and may have passed my gun off."

"Cindy? Who is she?"

"She was the girl who me and your father were fighting over. And I think she had something to do with everything. I heard that she and your father's longtime friend, Peanuts, were working together. Now I'm not saying he was involved. I'm saying that it's funny how he took over my territory so quickly with her help."

"Are you still in contact with her?" Dream asked.

"Naw. In the beginning she had come to see me a couple of times to act like she cared, but she stopped after a while."

"But why couldn't you fight in the trial, if you knew you didn't do it?

"I did try to fight it, but along with the gun were some witnesses who testified that they heard me say that I was gonna kill him. And given my reputation back then, it was believable to the jury."

"Why do I believe you?"

"Because truth never lies."

"Mr. Akbar, I took some courses in law and I know a little about the law somewhat. So I'm gonna dig a little deeper into this whole thing. If I find out who really killed my father, then I'll be back to see you and work on getting you out of here."

"Ms. Flowers, it's too late for that. I have a terrible record and I've done a lot of time. For the one thing I didn't do. So what I didn't get time for what I did do, I'm paying for it now."

"Bur you're initially here for killing my father right, and you've changed your life?"

"Correct."

"So there's a chance."

"A chance?"

"Like I mentioned, I know a little about the law. With what I know and me finding out who was really behind my father's death, there is a chance. Why do I like you? I don't know, maybe it's because I'm a dream come true."

Leaving the jail, Dream's head was spinning with confusion. For some reason, she had believed in what Mr. Akbar was saying. And what was this thing about this Cindy girl and my G-Daddy. What did he mean by he don't know if he had anything to do with it? Then there was some lady who tried to push my mother off the road. Why? So many things were going on. So many questions that demanded answers. And she was determined to get them.

She stopped home to freshen up before going back to see her mother. Inside the mailbox was something from FedEx addressed to her. She opened it and it was a CD with a letter on it reading "Listen to this." Just when Dream was about to listen to the CD, it was interrupted by a knock on the door.

"Who is it?"

She said in a disturbed voice.

"It's Kareem."

"Kareem!" she shouted. She opened the door and hugged her brother.

"So what's going on Lil Sis? How's Ma doing and how did this happen?" Kareem asked.

"I don't know, Reem. It's so much going on right now. Everything is crazy.

"The doctor who helped my mother out of the car said that he saw some lady deliberately trying to run my mother off the road. Like trying to kill her. Reem, what's going on?

"Then, I find out that my father was murdered instead of in a car accident. My mother lied to me. Did you know anything about this, Kareem?

"Yes, I did Dream," he answered.

"And you let me believe this my whole life? Why? Why did my mother lie to me?"

"I don't really know the reason, she just asked me to not talk to you about it if it ever came up."

"But I know now. And I went and spoke to the person who was supposed to have killed my father."

"You what? For what? For real?"

"Yes, I did. I needed to know something. And I believe he didn't do it."

"But it was said that his gun was the weapon."

"I know, he told me that. But he mentioned my G-Daddy and some chick named Cindy. He said that he don't think my G-Daddy had nothing to do with it, but this Cindy woman he thinks set him up."

"Wow. Word! So he did all that time for nothing, Kareem spoke.

"Yes it seems that way, at least for allegedly killing my father. Kareem what was my father and G-Daddy's relationship like?" Dream asked.

"They were the best of friends, I thought, at one time. Then when your father made it big, I don't think that they were that close anymore. Your father wouldn't let him be in his video. So Peanuts got mad. I think Peanuts was jealous of your father, if you ask me. Everybody showed your father more love than Peanuts.

"I think that by your father becoming successful and leaving the streets alone, Peanuts didn't like that, so they fell out after that. And to blow your mind a little bit more, if I'm right, I think that Cindy girl maybe the same Cindy that used to date your father."

"Huh? What you talking bout, Reem?"

"Yea, before your mother, he and this Cindy was together."

Dream was puzzled. The story was unfolding a little more each day. Every little piece of information was like piecing together a puzzle. She sat there and listened to her god-brother as her brain computed every bit.

When Kareem left, Dream remembered that she was about to listen to the CD. Eager to know what was on it, she placed it in the CD player to see why this was so important to listen to. As she listened to the two voices on the CD, Dream was devastated. She could not believe what she was hearing. It was the plot to kill her father.

It was all a horrible story to her and to have happened all in her birthday month. Wow! The man who she called G-daddy, her godfather, who gave her lavish gifts, who was there for her at times when she needed a father figure around. Who she was about to get a record deal with. This man, who she adored had stolen from her the one thing that could not be replaced. Her father.

Dream knew what she had to do., but she had nothing to do it with. She would make a pit stop just before going to Peanuts Productions.

At the same instant, a man dressed in a Fed Ex uniform walked in the DEA's office. He was slender in body weight, clean shaven, well-groomed to the tee. He wore glasses that made him look geekish.

"Excuse me. I am here to deliver a package for Tamika Brown."

"I can sign for it," the receptionist said.

"The person who it is for has to sign for it," he replied.

"No problem." The receptionist called for the agent.

About 5 minutes later, the beautiful agent, Tamika Brown, walked towards the FedEx man who was holding a package. She hasn't seen this one before and she knew all the regulars.

"Good evening. A package for me?"

"Yes ma'am. Sign here please." She signed for the package. It was very light.

"Thank you," she told him.

"You're welcome," the FedEx man replied. . He watched as she walked away, amazed at her walk.

SO THAT was the agent who has been obsessed with me for all these years," Luis Sanchez said to himself. He had wanted to meet her face to face, to be up close, to see what she was like, to sniff out her personality. That's why he had delivered the package, disguising himself as a FedEx man. He loved the cat and mouse game. And to stand right in front of someone who is out to get you, and they not even know it's you. That was a turn on for him. It gave him a sense of power. So to meet his obsession and to put in her hands the destruction of Peanuts and that bitch Cindy was perfect.

Agent Tamika Brown was in total shock of what she was hearing on the CD that came out of nowhere. She didn't know who sent it. It was addressed to her though. As if someone wanted to help her out or something because the CD had a big promotion sign on it. Well, it might have just as well had said that because she was going to get a big one, after her boss heard this. She sat back and smiled for a second. And then took off.

Dream walked inside the building of Peanuts Production studio carrying a small black Chanel bag just big enough to hold a few items. Given to her by her godfather, which was one of many birthday gifts from him. Birthday, she thought. This will be a birthday that she would never forget. As she got closer to the studio door, she heard two voices arguing back and forth. It was Peanuts and somebody. She walked in slowly.

"Dream," Peanuts shouted nervously. "What a surprise. Come in, come in."

Peanuts wondered how long she had been standing there and how much she heard.

"No need to stop on my account," Dream started. "Go ahead and continue. You were speaking about some lady you ran off the road."

"So what bitch if I was, what's it to you?"

"This is Dream, Cindy," Peanuts rushed to say.

"Ooooh so this is Dream, huh? Daddy's lil girl?"

"Yea, I'm Daddy's lil girl. And he wanted you two to listen to this."

Just then she handed Peanuts the CD of them all over it.

"What's this," Peanuts asked looking bewildered.

"Just Play it. It's a hit. That's why I came over. Just so that you can listen to it."

Peanuts put the CD inside of his device so that it could play out loud. Peanuts face just dropped. His whole body just slumped downward.

Cindy shouted out, "What the fuck? Where you get this from?"

Dream and Peanuts was just looking at each other. Peanuts was lost for words.

"Why godfather, Why?" she asked him as she started sobbing.
"Dream, I ..."

And before he could get anything out, she pulled out a nice handy 38 snug nose.

"Dream, hold on. Wait a minute. What you got that gun for? What you gonna do with that?" a nervous looking Peanuts shouted.

"Yea, you lil bitch. What the fuck you gonna do with that."

Dream aimed at the window and let go two shots. Then pointed the gun right back at them.

"What the fuck you think I'mma do? Y'all had my father killed and you, bitch, tried to kill my mother! Now how does it feel where your life is threatened?"

Dream was a good shot. Her boyfriend used to take her to the gun range on the regular so handling a gun was no problem. She never thought that it would come in handy one day.

The police, who were already in position to raid the building, heard the two shots and quickly dispersed into action.

"You stole from me the one thing that's missing from my life." She was holding the gun straight at Peanuts.

"Dream, hold on. Let me say something."

"There's nothing to say you piece of shit. You made me think that you was special. I called you G-Daddy for all those years. I loved you. And he was your best friend."

Dream was crying now. She was hurt that she had to kill this man, this man who had been there for her as a father. She was really hurt.

Just then, as she was still pointing the gun at him, a voice spoke out, "Don't do it Dream. It's not worth it. Put the gun down."

"No, they need to die. They killed my father," Dream said.

"I know," said the beautiful agent, Tamika Brown. "But not like this. Let the law handle it.

"What the..." a stunned Peanuts had to say.

"Anthony Robinson and Cynthia Smalls, you're under arrest for the murder of Michael Flowers."

Peanuts and Cindy could not believe what they were seeing, let alone hearing.

"Shay-Shay, you a fucking pig?" shouted Peanuts.

"Get the fuck outta here. This bitch a cop?" busted out Cindy. "You was playing us all along. You laid in my bed and acted like my woman. You stink ass bitch!" Exclaimed Peanuts.

"Trust me, it was a dirty ass job, but someone had to do it," said Agent Brown. She had loathed his kind, ever since her father was murdered. She didn't respect men who got rich off a substance that was harmful. She had been after this one and his boss for years. She had gone undercover as his girlfriend to do whatever it took to bring him down. They were too smart though. She didn't learn too much because Peanuts didn't tell his women nothing. And now she was about to arrest him for murder. Dream stepped back as she was witnessing her godfather get arrested.

"Oh come on now Shay-Shay. You don't wanna do this."

"Yes I do, and don't call me that, you fucking moron."

As they were going back and forth, Cindy saw an opportunity to reach in her back and pull out her nine millimeter.

"I'm not going nowhere," she shouted, but before she could even raise it up to fire off one shot, the agents that were with agent Brown were much quicker. As their aim was true, it hit its target on the spot. Cindy with blood gushing from her body, collapsed. She died instantly.

After the rupture of gunfire, the room went quiet for a second. Peanuts always had a loaded nine millimeter in his drawer but dared not to try anything after he witnessed the quick death of his friend. He had no choice but to surrender. AS the other agents handcuffed him, Agent Brown spoke to Dream, who was shaken up by the events that had just taken place.

"Are you all right, Ms. Flowers?"

162

"Yes, I'll be ok. Thank you." Dream replied.

"I'm so sorry for what happened to your father. He was a very cool dude. I got a chance to get to know him and he was ok."

More tears were coming out of Dream's eyes, as Agent Brown spoke.

"That's what people tell me," Dream said.

"I know it's hard on you finding out the truth about what really happened, but Peanuts will pay for his crime and more. So don't worry and take care of yourself."

"Thank you so much, and I will."

Dream watched as they put her godfather in the car and drove off. With him went her chances of becoming a big hit in the music industry. It had come that quick and went just as fast. Tomorrow was her 20th birthday, a birthday she would remember forever. She left to see how her mother was doing.

Inside was nothing new to Peanuts. He had been here before. But his status had some changes, since he became a businessman and being in there for the murder of a star. He was not placed in population. He sat back in his cell, wondering how the hell someone had recorded him and Cindy plotting to kill Daddy. He could only think of one person, Luis Sanchez. He wanted to get even. He would not sit back and let this man get the best of him. After all the money I made him. He knew too much not to get even. He thought to himself to tell everything he knew to strike a deal. He knew how bad they wanted him, so he would help them. Yep, he would talk to Shay-Shay. He sat back smiling. Just them, a guard knocked on the cell door.

"Chow time", he spoke out. He opened the window on the door and put a tray of food with coffee on the lid, so Peanuts, who was starving, took the tray and coffee, and started to eat. He was still talking to himself of how he was going to set Sanchez up, but as he drank the coffee, something wasn't right. Suddenly, he found himself losing oxygen. He started holding his throat, choking. Soon, nothing but white foam was coming from his mouth. The coffee was laced with cyanide. He died on the spot.

Tameka Brown stood looking out of her brand new office window. She had been promoted to a higher rank, but why was she not satisfied. She looked back at when she was a little girl. She could never forget that horrible scene when she was forced to watch her father and two others eat raw cocaine. This was why she had joined the force, to hunt down and catch this monster, but he had vanished yet again, leaving no traces behind. She had thought that Peanuts would be a big help, but he met his fate before she could even question him. She spoke out to no one, "I will get you, whatever it takes. I will get you!"

ROBERT JONES, AKA Stacks walked out of prison a free man. He had long done his time and then some for being in there for the murder of Daddy Flowers. He was let go because of Dream's promise to him; and he didn't do it, so they had to let him go. He walked out fresh as can be with a mindset to take back what he had, but little did he knew, "the game ain't da same".

Dream had just finished seeing her mother. She had told her everything that had transpired within the last few hours. It had been like a mini movie being played right in front of her, and she was the leading actress. But this was no movie, it was dead on real. While sitting there reflecting on the events, she didn't notice the mysterious-looking man who had snuck right beside her.

"Excuse me miss, do you know what time the bus arrives?" he asked. "It should be here in the next couple of minutes," she responded. "Yes I'm waiting on someone," he lied. "It's getting cloudy out, looks like it's going to rain. Are you visiting someone here at the hospital?" 'Yes, my mother." "How is she?" he asked. "She's doing much better than she was before; thank you for asking." "You're welcome," the mysterious man replied. "You have a beautiful voice, I heard you singing as I was walking up. Have you ever thought about singing as a career?" Dream looked at him with a puzzled look on her face as if she wanted to hear anything about singing as a career. She was well on her way, but that all came to a stop. Giving all that took place, she would have been a singing sensation by now. There's no doubt she would have made it! But the person that was going to put this all in motion was no longer her godfather, so that was that.

"I have thought about it once or twice, but nothing serious," Dream replied. "I mean with that voice there would be no problem getting a record deal! In my line of work I come in contact with a few people who know people. Maybe I can help you," he said. "I don't know," Dream said. "Well, I'll tell you what, here's my card; and if you decide to go with it give me a call." "I didn't even get your name." "I go by the name of Luis Sanchez."